Fitted Pieces

by Una Warde

Acknowledgments

To my parents, **Bridget** and **James**,

who encouraged me to be myself.

To **Robin**, who makes love real and each day an adventure. Her support and insight made the writing of this book possible.

To **Laura Kepner**, my writing mentor, a freelance writer and member of the Safety Harbor Writers and Poets Group. Her scholarly input provided much needed knowledge.

To complete a book, you need expert technical support and editing. Thank you **George Murphy** and **Harvey Balopole**, the Town Wizard.

To **Joanne Fried** who encouraged me to write my story.

I am also grateful to my life-long friend **Sindee Smolowitz** who read the book twice and provided editing and suggestions.

I thank my sister **Fran** who shared her memories and ideas.

And my friends Ellen, Laura, Liz and Terry, Eileen and Georgette for their ideas and support.

Return again, return again,

return to the land of your soul.

Return to what you are, return to who you are,

return to where you are.

Born and reborn again.

Lamentations 5:21.

Introduction

This is a book of fiction inspired by memory. The memories are poured into the pages through the sieve of my own experience and imagination and the storytelling of family and friends.

The story is about my unique journey, the evolution of my spirit. I write it with respect for those other paths I have crossed along the way, recognizing that each of us must find our own answers, our own truth. It is my hope that my journey will inspire yours.

Large fragments of time were hidden, partly through necessity and lack of choice but also at times through self-imposed caution and fear. Writing this book lifted the veil of illusion from the past.

In my 30s I fell in love with making stained glass pieces. Sand transformed from a solid to a liquid and back to a solid by fire. Each fragment makes little sense until fitted together as a whole. Each piece is scored and broken in the right places. Soldered together to tell a story. When light passes through the glass, it comes alive. Colors shift. Dark fragments accentuate the light ones. Different angles create shifting perceptions and an ever-expanding transparency. Patterns wander.

Never static, the same intricacies mimic our journey in life. Fragments of time fitted together. Dark times illuminate new experiences. Crimson shards bleed into opposites of bright yellow in the morning light. Illumination. Enlightenment.

Chapter 1

Thomas Michael, the beloved son of Bridget and Jim Walsh, died in 1947. He looked exactly like Jim as an infant. The golden, curly haired boy died of meningitis on the road to Dublin from the West of Ireland. The Athlone road cuts through the heart of Ireland, a treeless landscape, with bog lands and isolated farms. Medical services were limited in the West and the long journey along this road was their last hope. Bridget held their one and a half year old infant in her arms in the back seat of the old Ford as she watched him struggle for his life. It was too late. She was powerless to save him. Jim was powerless to save him.

"If only we were in America or Dublin, he would have lived," Bridget sobbed.

Jim wrapped his arms around her on the side of the road, as they both absorbed the horrible reality of their baby's death. No words could console them. This unbearable loss broke their hearts and marked the rest of their lives.

At the beginning of summer of that year they moved to the suburbs of Dublin with their two children, Grainne, age 3 and Gerard, age 13. The residents of Dun Laoghaire, a small town on the coast, were delighted to welcome the new Walsh grocery shop they opened that specialized in the finest of meats and food delicacies. A large living room, dining room and kitchen were in the back of the shop that opened onto a small garden filled with light in the early morning. Three bedrooms were on the second floor with windows facing either the front street or the garden area. It was a perfect setting to raise their young family, and the community of colorful characters who came to the shop loved the newcomers.

"It's been my dream to own my own business," Jim said, and Bridget understood.

Jim was supposed to inherit the family baking shop in the West of Ireland, where he started as an apprentice but to everyone's surprise, it was left to his two aunts. He never accepted nor understood this. While Jim and Bridget created a new life, they acknowledged to each other that "life would never be easy and the unexpected would most likely happen." A determination was set in their minds to make life better for their children.

The following year an early winter caught all of Ireland by surprise. The January newspapers hinted of a snowstorm of unusual strength. Those that could plan ahead did so with extra supplies of canned goods, boxes of oatmeal and coal. Neighbors promised to help each other. Shop customers were particularly concerned as Bridget was pregnant again and due to deliver at any time. Ned Devine, a member of the Garda, always neatly in uniform, couldn't live without Kelly's Irish sausages and imported chocolates.

"I'll be takin' ye to the hospital in Dublin no matter the weather," he said. "It will be a state of emergency and the police car will make it through any storm. It might give ye some peace to know, I have delivered a few babies in me time too. So not a worry on it!"

"Thank you, Ned. I hope we won't be needing an escort by the Garda but I'll definitely take you up on it if we need to," Jim replied. He handed him his neatly-packaged sausages in white paper with his weekly Irish lottery ticket.

Ned pushed closer to the counter and covered his mouth with the sausages. He whispered to Jim.

"Let's give this one a better chance of gettin' through the rough times, hey Jimmy. Ye got me at your back now."

A wink of the eye followed and the well meaning busybody of a man clanked the shop door behind him. Bridget overheard the conversation and came to Jim.

"What if something happens to this baby? I don't think I could bear it."

"We will be fine. We're in the great city of Dublin with the best of medical care in the Republic of Ireland. The snow won't stop us. Remember how we lived through that snowstorm in Manhattan?"

"How could I forget it? You slipped in your new galoshes on the steps that had totally disappeared with the snow. There were no trains. Cars were banned from the streets. Twenty-five years ago. I'll never forget the spirit of people in New York holding on to each other, helping each other."

"Oh, I remember the fall. My pride was hurt more than anything. Ireland may not know how to deal with snow Bridget, but we do. We'll get through this."

Mrs. O'Leary entered and stopped, as she always did, to inhale the sweet smell of Cadbury's chocolates on the shelf by the door.

"Intoxicating," she said. "Brings my childhood back."

She filled the space in front of the counter with her basket on one arm and her faun colored cocker spaniel called Biscuits in the other.

"When I enter your shop the aroma of fresh roasted coffee and chocolate arouses all my senses. It makes me want to fill my basket to the top. I need so many things," she said and pulled out a long list from her pocket. It wasn't clear if she really needed everything on her list or she just liked to prolong the visit with Bridget and Jim. She obviously needed the socialization and the good feelings of the shop. Biscuits was her only and truly loved companion.

"The Irish Times is predicting snow you know. Are you ready? I know I'm not. I keep making new lists. I have to worry about Biscuits too. He gets naughty if you change his routine or his food. I cook for him." She took a breath and looked at Bridget. "When is the baby coming? You must be worried sick. How are your other children, your handsome boy and lovely girl? Such a beautiful family you have." Another breath. Bridget reached to support her aching back as the rotund little woman rattled on without waiting for an answer.

"I am just two doors down from you if you need any help. You know if the baby comes suddenly. I don't have children of my own, ya know. Wasn't in the cards. I'd be delighted to help out."

When Jim got out of bed Tuesday morning, he pulled back the front bedroom curtains to see the entire street blanketed in snow. He shivered from the cold air seeping through the window and quietly slipped back into bed beside Bridget.

"The newspaper reports were right?" she asked as their eyes met and she took a deep breath to face the news. "We're covered in snow, aren't we? How will we get to the hospital? Let's look out the window together."

They quickly donned their dressing gowns and slippers. The window opened onto the front street after they removed clumps of snow. The familiar scene of shops and shutters facing them had disappeared. The rooftops blended with the white sky. White rolling hills replaced the familiar Packards and Fords that lined the sides of the street.

"Let's not wake the children yet."

Jim closed the window and without a sound, they crept down the stairs together.

"If we open the front door, the snow will fall into the house. There has to be a few feet already. I'll put on warm clothes, grab the shovel and tackle it. How about some warm tea?" said Jim.

While the teakettle boiled, Bridget turned on Radio Eireann to hear the weather. Their RCA tabletop wooden set glistened with newness. It started with a harsh hiss until she fine-tuned it to hear the booming voice of Prime Minister Eamon de Valera amid the constant crackle.

"I implore you citizens of Dublin and surrounding areas to stay behind closed doors. Do not go out into the cold and blasting snow. All trains have been shut down and government offices and schools are closed. Only emergency vehicles should be on the roads. Pray that this storm will end as quickly as it arrived."

Bridget covered her face with her hands as she absorbed the terrifying news. The words bounced off the walls and shot into her brain as her worst fears were aroused.

A reporter's voice followed, saying, "That was our Prime Minister urging great caution to the citizens of Dublin. If you can hear me, then you still have power wherever you are, but conditions can change rapidly." His voice picked up speed in order to deliver his message before a complete power failure. "An arctic blast has arrived through the night and plastered itself on every doorway, roadway, field and stream, every tree and mountain. Heed the cautions to stay indoors. Those able must do all they can to assist fellow citizens in this crisis as the government takes immediate action to clear the roads and help the needy. We will be reporting…" and the radio suddenly clicked off with a bzzt-baba-bzzt-baba-bzzzzzzzt sound. The teakettle sang on the stove and Jim's shovel crunched and scraped a pathway outside the shop door.

"We are truly at the mercy of Mother Nature with this one," Jim said as he brushed the snow off his clothes and stamped his feet on the shop floor. Prayers of the faithful were being said for sure but all the rosaries whispered behind these iced windowpanes would not be heard. The cold winds froze the muttered prayers mid-air.

"Holy Mary pray for us sinners now and at the hour of our death." Some believed that the wrath of God was being directed against Ireland.

Gerard, their first born thirteen-year-old son bounded down the stairs, overcome with excitement about the storm.

"Did you see what's outside the house?" he yelled. Bridget had to smile at his enthusiasm, and his jet-black uncombed hair flying in every direction above his boyish handsome face.

"We do indeed," replied Jim. "Schools are closed." Gerard punched his fists into the air, totally delighted with unexpected freedom.

"No exams this week! No football practice either!"

Gerard was named for his uncle, a psychiatrist who lived in Bath, England. The two were much alike in personality, full of exaggerated stories and antics, charming and smart in a roguish, unpredictable sort of way. Gerard knew at an early age that he would also become part of the medical profession, and with that gain a passport to Dublin society.

"I'm going to need your help in the shop moving merchandise to higher shelves and shoveling the snow so customers can get in." Jim was also anticipating the heavy rains and melting of snow that would follow when the warmer temperatures came.

"That's not going to be much fun for me," Gerard said, and slumped into the chair by the fireplace. "I don't want to be a grocery shopkeeper's helper."

But that he became, as the world he knew came to a complete stop. He would often disappear to his books of Irish poetry, an interest that would follow him into adult life.

Grainne came into the living room, wiping the sleep from her eyes and listening to Bridget explain the white world that suddenly appeared outside her window.

"It's beautiful: Can I go out and play in it?"

"In a few days you can."

"Where's my swing? I don't see it. Daddy, where is it?"

In the springtime Jim had made a swing for Grainne in the back garden but it was nowhere to be seen today. He quickly recalled the wild laughter of his daughter as he pushed her higher and higher in the warm summer air.

"We'll fix it when the storm is gone," he replied, staring out the window.

Grainne could not comprehend what had happened while she slept.

"And the birds are gone too," she exclaimed, turning to her mother for an answer.

"The birds had to leave Ireland for a warmer spot until it's over. They won't be singing as they usually do for a while. The birds will come back. I'll need you to help me until they do."

Grainne contemplated the situation and felt an early sense of seriousness and sudden loss of all that she knew. She helped in small ways, even as she clung to Bridget's skirts, upset but excited about the changes in her small world. She discovered a new art form by tracing her finger on the iced window panes, creating faces and images of trees blurred by the blinding snowfall. On some days the temperatures were so low, the panes were iced on the inside as well as the outside. She had unlimited canvasses for her creative imagination.

"Daddy, Mammy, come see the tree I made in my bedroom." A tall tree with graceful lines of a swing in motion through the frosty air filled the back garden window.

In her 3-year-old mind she wanted the pictures to last forever, but the chilling ice blurred them over and over and took them from her. This youthful experience stayed with her and gave her confidence as an artist in her adult years.

Jim and Bridget were worried about many things. They were worried about how their small family and the grocery store would survive this sudden and scary blizzard. What if their extra supply of turf and coal was not enough? We'll have to use it sparingly. There would be no milk bottles delivered to the shop door and the bread truck would not be on the road for a long time. What if the electrical lines become frozen and we lose electricity? What new troubles would the morning bring?

These things they could handle. What was terrifying was how they would get to the hospital if the baby came. Would she have to deliver her child at home during this storm? Would the baby survive?

Ned Devine's long-nosed skinny face appeared in the shop door window. He wiped the frost away and pushed the door, almost falling into the shop as he opened it. Beneath his old tweed overcoat, he wore his Garda uniform, ready to serve, ready to help. He stomped great lumps of snow off his boots.

"How are things?" he asked. "Are ye all right? It's penetrating cold, 'tis. Slaps you on the face 'tis so full of ice. The boyos are out with tractors on the roads already, ploughing as best they can. The inventions for pushing the snow to the side of the road are amazing. Big scoops attached to the front end. It's awful heavy this stuff. Bitter cold! Bitter cold!

Any stirrings from the baby, Bridget? I'm here to drive you with an escort to the hospital through this sea of snow whenever you need me."

Bridget cradled her stomach with those kind words. "Thanks, Ned. We will call on you if we have to."

"You did a good job on the front walk, Jim. A fine ditch you made. I'm off to help shovel down the road. Una Brady fell into a drift while trying to get to work this morning on her way to the clothing factory. Almost lost for good if it wasn't for a young fellow pullin' her out. She wasn't going to risk the new job by not showin' up."

Ned flicked the Player's cigarette he had been smoking into the snow as he left the shop; shovel in hand, bound by duty. He tilted his head downward and wrapped the scarf tightly around his face and headed past the window. The snowflakes fought each other as they fell in all directions against the shop window and on Ned's Garda cap, securely fastened by his chinstrap.

The storm abated through the night. Jim and Bridget lay beneath the covers, closer than ever, exchanging body heat and summoning the necessary strength to survive. It was often beneath the covers that their prayers were answered. The early morning winds announced more snow was on the way and a new day began with the sound of falling ice and shovels hard at work in the street below.

Chapter 2

A loud knock on the shop door that morning brought everyone running. Kevin Lenahan, a schoolmate of Gerard, jumped up and down outside the doorway to keep warm. Gerard jerked the door open. He recognized the Irish knit hat pulled over his friend's ears. His bushy, blond eyebrows were frosted over. The heat of his breath was visible when he shouted from a slit in his scarf wrapped in triplicate around his rotund face. His already enormous physique filled the narrow walkway between the snow walls Jim had made. He clutched a gardening shovel in one hand.

"We're forming a gang, a brigade to work in the storm. We need you to join us."

Knowing they could not contain Gerard with his schoolmate at the door, Jim and Bridget let him loose. He bundled up with all he could find, including an old overcoat from his Uncle Gerard, and vanished out the door.

The boys headed towards their usual hangout, the Forty Foot near the Martello Tower in Salthill. After two hours they reached the spot where they felt like gods. Gentlemen only could bathe freely here and the boys dove into the water in all kinds of weather, just not today. James Joyce penned the opening scenes from Ulysses at the top of the tower. They entertained images of Leopold Bloom, an ordinary Jewish man and hero of the book, and Stephen Dedalus, a radical irreligious youth, struggling to find his identity. There was no climbing to the top of the tower today to see the panoramic view of Dublin. The tower was built by the British to defend against French attacks. The only view today would be of whitewashed land in all directions. Heading home after a snowball fight, he and his friends were happy to have put a few shillings in their pockets, shoveling a shop doorway or delivering hand written messages on foot. They were a smart and inventive group able to assemble makeshift sleighs from discarded items at home. In the days ahead they drove them through the snowy streets, delivering supplies and newspapers for the small town south of Dublin.

Back at the grocery shop Bridget, in her 9th month of pregnancy, was still taking orders. Customers started to make their way to the shop. Today felt different. The baby moved more and more.

"Oh, oh, I just got kicked," she exclaimed and braced herself on the counter. She handed the Dominican Sister her bottle of Irish cream and pound of imported coffee.

"Will you be wanting me to fetch your husband? Is the baby coming? Oh Jesus, Mary and Joseph in this snow! The Holy Couple did make it to Bethlehem though, didn't they now? That's a consoling thought, Bridget."

Sister Mary Theophane, a Dominican nun from the private Catholic school up the road, was a regular customer. Every conversation was an opportunity to spread a message of hope and belief in the Church.

"The nuns will say a special novena for you this evening. The Blessed Mother will watch over you."

She looked towards the heavens as she stepped into the fresh falling snow as though the sun was shining and the snowstorm was a figment of everyone else's imagination.

Bridget sat down with her favorite cup of Bewely's Afternoon Tea, her shop apron lifted high on her protruding abdomen.

Grainne came running in from the back of the house, out of breath.

"Mammy, Mammy, it started snowing again. Can I please go out in it?" Bridget held her stomach as Jim arrived back from shoveling the street.

"Are you okay? Do we need to go to the hospital?"

He saw her changed expression of pain and anxiety. Sweat glistened on her forehead.

"You shouldn't be working in the shop. Is Gerard back yet?"

"No, Jim, he's still out. The baby is kicking. I'm scared of driving in this storm but I think we need to go."

"Well, the bloody snow started again, so we better get ahead of it."

Gerard burst through the back door, his clothes soaked through and his face flushed with the cold.

"Gerard, go tell Ned we need him immediately. You will need to take care of Grainne. Your Mom and I are going to the Rotunda Hospital now."

Within minutes Ned Devine was in the middle of the road in his Ford Anglia, lights flashing and horn blasting. A second Garda car appeared ahead of them as Jim helped Bridget into the back seat and squeezed in next to her. The car in front began to move and the Garda siren wailed like an opera singer changing her notes. All activity stopped on the street and shouts of "Good luck" and "God speed" were barely audible. This was not how they expected to bring their next child into the world. They were in Ned's hands now. Fear filled the car. Ned was calm and drove hunched over the steering wheel. He took the old tram road, through Blackrock toward the heart of Dublin, undaunted by poor road conditions. It would take them much longer to drive the eight miles from Dun Laoghaire to Parnell Square in the south of Dublin.

He was an excellent driver. He followed the escort car at just the right distance to avoid a direct collision. Driven by the fierce winds, the snow slanted through the headlight beams. Jim and Bridget held on tight to each other. The death of their baby son weighed heavily on their minds tonight as much as on the day he died along the Athlone road to Dublin.

Ned glanced at them in the rear view mirror. "The old tram road is safer than the new one, less twists and turns."

"Wouldn't the new road be faster Ned?" asked Bridget.

"Ah not at all. Not at all. The lorries are trying to make deliveries even in this weather and they have to take the new road. Better to avoid them entirely."

Suddenly one of the snow-caked wipers doing overtime broke in half. Ned carefully applied the brakes and pulled to the side of the road. The car in front stopped. Jim jumped from the back seat and pulled off his glove and stuck it on the broken wiper.

"Masterful," said Ned as Jim slammed the door closed and they cautiously drove on. "Masterful. It's wavin' us on to safety."

The rhythmic motion of the glove mimicked the contractions in Bridget's uterus. She found herself making short panting breaths in timing with the glove. The chill in the car turned her puffs into visible crystals in the air.

"The glove's not bad at all, is it?" asked Jim.

She answered with an ooooooh and aaaaaaah and tried to relax. One of the gloves she had given Jim in New York many years before was actually helping her. As they turned onto O'Connell Street Bridge, the car slipped and slid toward the riverside. Jim immediately put his arm in front to protect her and she fell sideways into his body. The mother of pearl rosary beads she held tightly in her hand fell to the floor.

"Hang on," Ned shouted. He steered the car into the curve. Both of their bodies lunged forward and Bridget said, "Oh God! Oh God!" Ned was cursing as hard as any sailor, determined to regain control of his ship. The car grazed the street lamp on the right but within seconds was back in the middle of the street. The driver in the lead car saw the whole thing but continued to move slowly forward. All three breathed a sigh of relief.

"That sure was a close one," Jim said. "Are you okay, Ned?"

"Ah sure, nothin' to it, nothin' to it! We'll be at the Rotunda in a few minutes."

As Jim and Bridget sat back and tried to relax, they looked out on the City of Dublin, the 18th century Georgian architecture stripped away by the snow. Balustrades and finials that should have been visible were gone. The trees bowed their heads in compliant reverence. The hard edges of Dublin had vanished. These were the same streets that had witnessed invasions and rebellions, proclamations and bloodshed, victories and defeat. But tonight Ned Devine was conquering these treacherous streets. Bridget absorbed the chaos of creation descending on the city and then felt the kick of new life through her left hand while she clung to Jim with the other.

Ned crunched onto Parnell Street and parked in front of the main building of the Rotunda Hospital. It took four times the amount of time it normally would.

"We made it. Ned, you are the best. We owe you," said Jim.

Ned's official boots sunk into the icy snow as he opened the back car door for Jim and Bridget. Near the entrance crowds were exiting from the Gate Theatre, built beside the hospital in 1928. They chatted about the show, laughed in the snowy night air, oblivious to the cold. The show was a preview of *Where the Stars Walk*, a modern comedy written and performed by Michael Mac Leamour. He was one of the Gate Theatre founders and artistic director, along with his equally talented partner and lover, Hilton Edwards. They lived an openly gay lifestyle in moralistic Dublin. The play's origin was from a first play by William Butler Yeats called *The Land of Heart's Desire*. Here death and pain do not exist in a world of faeries.

Bridget's pain was definitely worsening with each contraction, each careful step forward. Jim gave a young couple his approving smile as they shouted back, "Congratulations." Wearing their Wellingtons, Jim and Bridget walked across the hospital's black and white patterned floor, leaving puddles in their paths.

A young plump nurse greeted them and quickly brought them to the first floor maternity ward.

"You've picked a grand night for having a baby, Mrs. Walsh," she stated in a lilting Dublin accent. "Nothing like a snow storm to get the contractions going! We'll take good care of you. My husband calls himself a "weather prophet" and predicted this very night to all the family just as the ham was passed to his plate at Christmas dinner. None of us paid any attention to him as he topped off his drink for a third time. He works for the new Weather Bureau in Dublin. He tells me the pressure in the air during a storm can make a woman's water break ahead of time. I got the smartest one in the whole family." Perhaps sensing she might be talking too much to the newly admitted and about to be new parents, she added, "The mid-wife will be with you in just a few minutes. We'll take very good care of you and your baby" and rushed out of the room as the only way to stop talking.

Bridget wasn't smiling as she squeezed Jim's hand, glad that the chatter had stopped.

"The nurse was right. I hope they come soon." At that very moment her water broke and gushed onto the sheets.

Jim heard voices in the corridor, relieved that help was on the way. He wiped the sweat from his brow as the white-coated male mid-wife entered the room with the night sister for the maternity ward.

"I'm Doctor Browne, the midwife and I see there is no need to tell you...you are in labor." Jim kissed Bridget on the cheek.

"I'll be right outside." He left the room reluctantly.

He stepped through the high columned doorway into the chapel to wait and calm his nerves. Jim imagined the echo sounds of concerts performed long ago within these same walls. For two hundred years, the likes of Haydn and Handel played in the ball-rooms and in the strolling gardens surrounding the hospital, for the Dublin elite.

I remember when the Gate Theatre opened. I took Bridget to see a play when we got back from America. We had such a great time that night.... A Mid-wife.... I wish he were a real doctor...

Jim was unaware of how the practice of midwifery had advanced. It was nevertheless controversial within the very walls of the Rotunda, or the Lying-In-Hospital as it was called in the past. A battle of the sexes raged over who was more qualified to care for women in childbirth; women who employed natural methods passed down through generations, or male doctors with formal medical education. Male midwives were treated with ridicule by their physician colleagues and were on the lowest rung of the medical ladder. They were often pictured in cartoon-like images of a half-female/half-male body.

The Rotunda is the best hospital for delivering a baby. It's been around for over two hundred years. They know what they're doing. I'm sure of that. She's in good hands. She is. I know she is. I wish I could pray like other people.

Jim gazed at the large richly decorated stucco ceiling and became lost in its beauty for a few moments. Statues of Faith, Hope and Charity reached into the open space above him. His eyes followed the golden vines and flowers until stopping at the depiction of Charity as a mother with a child at her breast. Feeling more relaxed, he dozed off until awakened by the light touch of the night sister an hour later in her crisply starched white apron, blue dress and a cap closely resembling a fluted cake dish.

"You can go to Bridget now," she said. "You have a lovely, healthy baby girl."

Born just minutes after midnight in a blizzard on January 19, 1948, a baby entered the world.

Jim hurried to Bridget's side, beaming with pride and love. He bent over to kiss her lying in the bed exhausted and holding their new daughter in her arms.

"We'll call her Maeve, like we said."

"Huh huh hwaaaaah! Myaaaaah! Ehhhh!"

"She has a fine set of lungs," Jim said.

And so I, Maeve Walsh, was set adrift, separated from my home of nine months, into the exciting adventure called life. Queen Maeve of Connaught lived in the first century and was known as one of the most powerful of Irish women. Some thought of her as a Celtic Goddess. It was a good name to be given.

The drifting snow and winds pelted the hospital windows for another two days and then stopped. Jim, my father, walked the six streets from his friend Richard's house on O'Connell Street for the first three days and then hopped on a CIE public transport lorry taking needed supplies south to Dun Laoghaire.

"You should stay with me Jim," Richard told him on the phone the day before they had to drive to the hospital. Friends and family extended themselves to help in any way. "All should be well with this one. It's time to move on from Thomas Michael," he added.

Mrs. O'Leary met him at the shop door, her apron caked with flour and the smell of Irish soda bread emanating from the kitchen. A streak of chocolate smeared her upper lip.

"I heard all about it from the neighbors. All is well. We did fine here. Gerard was a dear and Grainne and Biscuits are inseparable. I came over right after you left."

With that she gave him a big hug, sharing the remains of her cooking on his black overcoat.

Bridget stayed in the hospital for the normal long ten days. A winter sun shone, melting the accumulated snow and slowly permitting life to return to normal. Jim drove Maeve and Bridget home to Dun Laoghaire. Gerard brought home the newspapers with headlines that read, "Ireland Survives Another Treacherous Snowstorm," referring to the Arctic Siege of 1947 that lasted for months. During that storm many people died in the tenements of the city and in the countryside. Sheep were buried alive. Hospitals were overcrowded with broken bones and frostbite.

"I'm glad this storm was not like the last one," Jim said as the family gathered around the fireplace, taking turns holding the new addition to the household.

"I'm your older brother Gerard...I mean, much older brother. Old enough to be your father. I'll be teaching you a lot in the years ahead."

Grainne held the baby in her lap, delighted to have a new playmate, even if she was four years younger. "Where's her hair?" and "Why is she so wrinkled?"

"It's been a tough few weeks but we survived it. The shop will pick up business again in the days ahead. I admit I was frightened on the way to the hospital," said Bridget.

"But here we are together as a family."

The experience forged once again a Walsh family value that settled in the children's minds for the remainder of their lives. "When you are challenged or when something fails, you move on and do your best for the future." It permeated Maeve's beginning moments of existence.

Chapter 3

"Grainne, wake up, wake up," Gerard whispered in her ear. "Everyone is sleeping. I have a game for us outside in the snow." Grainne jumped out of bed.

"Here, put these clothes on and the gloves. Be quiet so we don't wake them."

He placed a pillow on the steps to the first floor to soften the noise, step after step as Grainne descended the stairs.

"What is it?" she asked excitedly, overjoyed to be in cahoots with her older brother and going into the snow.

There was a great snow-packed hill in the back garden and Gerard helped Grainne to the top.

He produced a brass-serving tray with handles that Bridget used for company.

"Sit on it and hold onto the handles tight. I'll push you down the mountain."

Grainne shivered with cold and excitement, enjoying every descent to where she landed outside the kitchen door. She could not suppress a shriek as the tray was going faster and faster with each ride.

"Aiieee!" shattered the cold air and in seconds Jim and Bridget arrived at the back door.

"What on earth? Get inside the house immediately! Grainne could have been hurt, Gerard," said Bridget. "And my good tray."

"Jobs for you today in the shop, my boy," said Jim.

He did them cheerfully. The excitement of the morning had been worth it.

The snow began to melt and the expected flooding saturated the gardens and houses, especially near the rivers flowing through Dublin. An early Spring arrived and the newly bloomed Bells of Ireland competed with the musty smell of stained garden walls. While all was returning to normal in the seacoast town of Dun Laoghaire, it would take many weeks for the land to dry.

"Once again De Valera has let us down," Bridget remarked at dinnertime.

Eamon De Valera, the Prime Minister of Ireland was much criticized for his handling of this snowstorm as well as the devastating blizzard of 1947. Bridget was a staunch Irish Republican and supported a united Ireland as an independent country. Many felt De Valera sabotaged the cause for independence from Britain in his lack of action and attendance at the Treaty Agreement of 1921. The Prime Minister had pledged the peaceful unification of Ireland, but it never happened. He shocked the people when he visited the German embassy to pay his respects on the death of Adolf Hitler in May of 1945.

He explained, "It is my diplomatic duty."

Jim and Bridget questioned his ideals and true revolutionary motives.

"Was he really a Hitler supporter? What side of the alliance was he really on?"

Discussions of this type were common and served to educate, indoctrinate and influence the children's growing awareness of Irish politics, religion, and democracy in America. They discussed their vulnerability in a country unable to take care of its people in an emergency. The newspaper headlines once again posted, "Government Officials Totally Unprepared." People died in tenements and it seemed everyone was left to their own devices to survive. In the coming years their love/hate relationship with Ireland would become more complicated, with hopes raised and then dashed, and with the growing need for more predictability in their daily lives.

The world into which I was born was one dominated by the clergy that held the reigns of power over politics and the intimacy of family life. Jim and Bridget did not escape the traditional messages from the Catholic Church on raising children or on spousal roles. She was the wife and mother and he was the husband, father and breadwinner. In a country so devoted to religious adorations, it was easy for Jim to adore Bridget. While he did not believe in Catholic teachings, he did believe in love. He was a romantic. Bridget was a devout Catholic, raised to believe in the teachings of the Church. Her faith gave her strength. They had true love and respect and simply accepted their differences. Children were to be seen and not heard, waiting to be spoken to with visitors, having table manners at every meal and never using even the slightest of bad language.

Within such a conservative country like Ireland, only the strong and rebellious spirits survived the brainwashing. An undercurrent of rebelliousness ran through the Walsh family. Would the pressure to conform be defeated by that undercurrent in the years ahead?

Mom told me the story of my baptism in the church in Dun Laoghaire. This sacramental initiation as a child of God into the Catholic Church was not a simple affair. The pouring of water on my bald head three times to cleanse me of original sin was witnessed by fifty school children as a Catechism lesson. They stood on the wooden seats to view the baptismal font and the small baby in the priest's oversized hands, giggling and pointing and falling into each other. My godparents, Eve and Gerard, held me as the cold water was poured on my forehead.

"Waa, waah, wah," I wailed, drowning out the explanation of the sacrament by the priest. It was a done deal with a host of witnesses.

Marked with the sign of the cross, the words were spoken, "I baptize you in the name of the Father, the Son and the Holy Ghost."

I was cleansed. If I died, I would go straight to heaven.

I don't remember much of what happened before the age of four. After that the grocery shop became my playground, especially in the mornings during the busy time. I fit just behind the counter, able to peek through the display glass at the different customers. If ever there was an arena for studying people and Dad interacting with them, this was it. He knew everyone's name and what they liked. Special orders were ready and waiting.

When Mrs. O'Leary bustled into the shop, I held my breath.

Every time she would ask, "How is my little sweetheart, Maeve?" At the sound of my name I would crouch down on my seat, hoping she wouldn't see me. Her dog Biscuits knew I was behind the counter and kept sniffing in my direction.

"Biscuits, settle yourself down now," she would say, not realizing the dog was on to something . . . me behind the counter.

"Oh, 'ello Jim dear. What a beautiful day," she would begin in her high-pitched voice. The words shot out from her round red lips, a little hole barely visible between her puffy cheeks. Dad always gave her a big smile and patted the dog's head. In between ordering the black pudding and Irish bacon for breakfast for two, she would talk about how fat Biscuits was getting, the newspaper headlines and any recent gossip she gathered from the neighbors.

"The Donovans are fighting again like cats and dogs. She threw him out on the street the other night into the snow. Poor man. He headed straight back to The Jaunting Car Pub on the corner to have another pint."

One day an English man came in with a strong accent wearing funny pointed shoes.

"A pack of Players, please," he chimed. I mimicked him exactly from my hiding place. The man laughed at my imitation of him but Dad apologized and whisked me out of the shop for the day. I caught a slight smile on his face though.

When I could, I would arrange the sweet tins on the shelves so my favorite was just a hand reach around the door. When the shop was busy I took handfuls of sweets like gobstoppers, seen only by the customers who couldn't help but smile. This alerted Dad who ran after me and interrupted my intended feast. On weekends Grainne and I went to the park with our au pair and made daisy necklaces sitting on the grass. I brought my favorite doll along whose head I could totally unscrew and look inside.

Grainne was not happy with this enjoyment of mine, as I commandeered her dolls to do the same.

"Why do you have to do that?" she asked. "The head is supposed to stay on the doll. You're wrecking them. I'm going to tell Mammy."

Gerard was on his path to become a doctor. As long as he passed his exams, he was left to his studies. The family catered to him as the firstborn male, and after Thomas' death, the only male child. But the reality of a sister fourteen years younger and another ten years younger, did not sit well with him. He had to share the spotlight. He spent most of his home time studying in his room. It had maps of the human body on the wall and a full size skeleton dangling from the ceiling. Sometimes he didn't mind if I visited and touched the bones to make it move about. He showed me the inside of a skull sitting on his desk with parts of the brain labeled in black ink.

When I was about six and had satisfied myself with his collection, I accidentally locked myself in the bathroom by his room on the second floor. The doorknob broke off and Gerard heard the rattling of my failed attempts to get out.

"Maeve, listen to me and do exactly what I say. Step on the toilet and climb out the window onto the roof. I'll go outside and catch you when you jump off."

I climbed out and there he was standing beneath the roof.

"Now bump yourself down the roof and jump off into my arms."

I was very scared but trusted him and did what he said. Just as he caught me in mid air, Mom came running out to see what the thumping noise was over the kitchen. Was she mad.

"Gerard, she could have been badly hurt."

"I knew I could catch her. Just like I do at football."

On another day he tied a rope around Grainne's waist and told her to use her feet on the side of the house as though she was climbing up a wall. He would at the same time pull her up with the rope into his room. It seemed like an adventurous new game and she did it. Mom, horrified once again intercepted him, as Grainne was more than half way up the house. She finished her ascent.

That evening Dad took the future doctor aside and had a long talk with him about endangering his sisters' welfare for his own amusement.

He yelled, "What is your fascination with roofs and ropes? They are your sisters and you need to protect them. Last week you tied Grainne up outside and left her there while she was trying to get out. Luckily Mrs. O'Leary saw her from her bedroom window after Biscuits heard her crying. Never again. Never again. Do you hear me?"

"Yes, Dad. I didn't mean any harm."

Within a few years, Gerard began the medical program at University College Dublin or UCD as it was called. The other choice was Trinity College, but a Catholic could not attend without special permission from their bishop. The archbishop enforced this old rule, calling it "an ungodly bastion of Protestant thought."

A story is told about a teaching doctor at Trinity in the 19th century who told the class on the first day that he did not teach 'niggers, Jews or Papists'. If any were present, "they should leave now." Many present had to leave before the lecture could begin.

We saw less and less of Gerard as he became more involved in his studies and college life. As the youngest child, I had a general sense that no one was watching me too closely. My elder siblings paved the way for my independence. Mom and Dad had their hands full working in the shop twelve hours a day. My sister and I attended the Dominican School, an uppity private school for girls in Dun Laoghaire.

Sister Imelda was the principal and exemplified the stern disciplinarian stereotype of a nun. Her elongated head was encased in a tight-fitting wimple of starched linen. Her black veil and habit surrounded her form as rosary beads and an enormous crucifix dangled from her well-hidden hips. Everyone feared her, even the other sisters. Her venom would erupt for the most minor of infractions.

"Miss Walsh, where is your beret? You are out of uniform," she said as she punched me down the stairs.

The other nuns were kind and pretty and made up for her nasty disposition. Sister Dymphna was young and beautiful and always greeted me with a big smile. These were women with power and unquestioned authority. Early on in life I experienced their strength, their learnedness, their forgiveness, their bond of sisterhood, their secrecy and hiddenness.

"Maeve, you're not supposed to touch sister's habit. It's sacred."

To my young and impressionable mind, this was seductive. The nuns targeted certain students to believe they could have a vocation to religious life, a calling like them to lead a secret life of service to God.

Dad and I talked about all matters of importance while I was growing up. When I was eight, we went for one of our usual hand in hand walks together in Dun Laoghaire. We strolled up the hill by the library when I made the announcement,

"You know, I am going to become a nun."

He stopped short on the street and looked directly at me.

He said, "It will be a blue moon the day you enter the convent."

His skepticism hit me hard since I had imagined he would be pleased for me to choose such a lofty goal. I was intrigued by his phrasing, "it will be a blue moon" as I did not fully understand what it meant. My imagination was captured with a new purpose. I would make that "blue moon" day possible. We walked on saying no more about it. Later on I learned blue moon meant something absurd or rare. As I look back on that small but significant talk, I am struck by how we all have been affected by such defining moments . . . times when we were forever turned in a certain direction or purpose that was to influence the entire course of our lives. Caught by our own volition, words spoken in the moment take up residence in our psyche.

So life began in a working class family with high ideals and standards. I saw a family portrait originally displayed on the mantelpiece of our small living room in Ireland. It was in color, framed in a simple eight-and-a-half by eleven black frame. Everyone was looking directly at the camera, through the lens into the empty space of their own future. The moment captured the uncertainty, hopefulness, sadness and resignation of the subjects. Mom and Dad were in the background sitting on the cranberry colored couch with matching corded fringes at the bottom. On either side of the couch were white marble side tables. The drapes had an attractive box design and were closed behind us, giving the room a sophisticated modern look.

My parents had the look of a fashionable Dublin couple. She was in a mid-length shift dress with matching jacket and he in a double-breasted pin stripe suit with cuffed pants. A beautiful leaf-shaped broach adorned Mom's jacket. Dad's arm rested around Mom. He smiled his familiar enigmatic smile. Mom's cheeks were flushed and she looked proud and happy. To their left was Granny Meehan, Mom's mother from the West of Ireland. She looked through her black-rimmed glasses with a steady, strong, concerned look. Her clasped hands lay together on her lap. She wore a black dress with white trim on the wrists and collar. To her right was Gerard in a navy blue suit and tie, knees crossed, acutely aware of his good looks. Grainne and I were seated next to each other on the floor in our best dresses, hands beneath the frills. Her hair was fair and curly; mine was jet black with straight bangs. She had a slight smile, while I was very serious. I was nine and she was thirteen. This was the only picture of everyone together that I have ever seen.

The photograph documented us at a turning point in the Walsh family history. Dad was leaving for America to prepare the way for us to follow. The grocery store had lost its edge despite the hard work, as the economy of Ireland was failing terribly. America was the answer as it had been for generations of Irish, forced to leave in order to build a stronger future for their family. Gerard would stay in Ireland to complete his medical studies. Granny would return to the West of Ireland with my uncle William who was the photographer.

How can they uproot me like this? What about my friends? I don't want to leave Ireland for some strange land. It's fine here. Have they gone mad?

I was miserable.

Before Dad left for America he gave me a gift of a glass globe on a black marble base and inside it was a small house surrounded by trees with a girl at the door.

"Shake it," he said.

Small white flakes suddenly started to whirl around the house and the girl until they hid the scene entirely and then slowly began to settle.

"You were born in a snowstorm you know. Anytime you want, you can create your own world and watch it change just by shaking it."

"I love it. It's magic, Daddy."

"I know you don't want to leave Ireland and everyone you know here. I think you will come to like America too. You'll make your own world there. Just like the snow globe does when you shake it."

Chapter 4

Knowing that I was leaving Ireland for good had a number of effects on my young psyche. Everything I did became magnified and more important because I would be doing it for the last time.

"Mammy, this will be my last chance to go to the big shops in Dublin. You have to take me with you. I'll never see Moore Street again with the wagons in the street . . . and the dancing skeletons. They won't have that in America . . . It's the last of the dancing skeletons for me. Daddy told me before he left that I could go to the cinema with my best friend Sean. I'll never have that chance again. We both saved our money to go. This will be my last summer in the country with my cousins. I'll never see them again."

Ireland and particularly the West of Ireland are full of wonder, myth, legend and fairy-tales. It was hard for me to imagine how my family could leave all this beauty behind.

During that last summer in Ireland I spent time in these special places, knowing it would be a long time in the future before I would see them again.

Loggathalan, which means "soft ground," was my very own beach. On warm days my cousin and I rolled our bathing suits into towels tucked beneath our arms and off we went. The long walk to the water's edge meandered through field after field and passed by the original Meehan house site. My uncle took large stones from the site and placed them in the house that now stands just beyond the Crossroads. We changed behind the Precambrian boulders and then ran into the water. The air smelled faintly of iodine as the seaweed washed about our feet. The hedges surrounding the small private sea alcove were full of giant fuchsia flowers, bending over like full crimson skirts bobbing in the wind. Cows called to us in the fields just beyond our sight. The young calves produced high-pitched bleats or bawls when they wandered too far away from their mothers or sensed our presence nearby, laughing and screaming in the water.

Mulranny was a half hour drive from the Crossroads by the house. "Maoil raithne" means "hill of the ferns." The seacoast village developed with the arrival of the Westport- Achill railway line in the 1890s. Mulranny beach was full of perfectly round smooth rocks, with the grand, old hotel standing on the hill overlooking the promenade to the sea, waiting for visitors to return. When I was there as a child, the sheep wandered on the beach and around the hotel grounds. They were our tour guides.

Sheeaun or Síodhán meaning "a fairy mound" or where the fairies lived, was one of my favorite little spots. You had to discover the exact hills where the fairies lived beneath the grass in order to see one. Dad told me to put my ear to the ground and very quietly listen in order to hear them beneath the surface. They were very clever at avoiding being seen by humans.

"There, I hear them playing music and dancing," I swore one day to my cousin.

"You don't," she said, as she jumped down beside me and we listened together.

We never actually spoke to one or saw one, but we knew they were there. You could see their paths around a few of the hills; small foot prints like a bunny or hare, left behind for us to run riot with our imaginations.

Achill Island, on the West Coast of Co. Mayo, was a full day trip that usually happened when visitors came to Derradda. The Atlantic Drive took us past spectacular rhododendron plants on the first part of the trip with fuchsia and bracken breaking out on the side of the road the further along you drove. The sun shone each time, regardless of the season. Craggy looking fisherman pulled on their nets by their colorful boats. Sheep balanced on treacherous cliffs. Herds of sheep often blocked the roadway as we drove to the very end of the Island. Achill, wild and remote, ended at a small, protected beach with cliffs rising on two opposite sides as the Atlantic waters washed gently onto the shore. An abandoned one-room stone house still stands with a glassless window overlooking the blue ocean.

Who lived in such a simple house, away from the rest of the world?

Beauty and majesty flooded within its humble walls.

Centuries earlier, Carrickahowley Castle was built by Granuailel, the Irish Sea Queen, to ward off British invaders. She was known as "the most notorious woman in all the coasts of Ireland." The key to the castle could still be found in a crevice by the door. We slid the lock open and had the entire castle to ourselves.

"Let's climb this circular staircase to the top," my cousin Mary shouted as she put one foot on the cold stone steps reaching to the second floor.

A round stone hole at the top of the stairs was the toilet they used that dropped human waste to the river beneath. We would sit on the toilet and laugh at what was our first experience of efficient outdoor plumbing. Then we peered through the thin window slits that accommodated the firing of guns at approaching vessels and marveled that a woman would have such strength and command of men. We imagined ourselves commanding and protecting the rugged coast of Ireland from foreign invaders.

"Leave these shores or risk dying this very day," we shouted.

Derradda is Gaelic for The Long Wood, which was where my grandmother's house was built. The house is where my mother was born and it's where my favorite aunt and uncle and cousins lived. The Gaelic word goes a long way back, since none of my cousins remember a wood anywhere near the house. It was my summer place. It was the place where my sister and I always felt we came from, even though we were not born there. Derradda is the one place in the entire world that continues to ground me through life. It's the place of my roots. The memory of happy childhood summer holidays and the images that collected in my mind remained undiminished as I aged.

The light in the back of the house blanketed the lake and the fields that led down to it. Newly mowed grass filled the air.

Tires crunched on the stones covering the boreen, letting us know visitors had arrived.

Turf fresh from the bog warmed the house.

Unrelenting offers of tea and the taste and smell of freshly baked Irish soda bread.

The West of Ireland has the most amazing stonewalls. They run zigzag through the fields, forming natural irregular boundaries. Each stone was placed by hands long ago, carefully and strategically, one on top of the other. These hands were cut and bruised, leaving their own marks. Blotches of white and yellow lichen settled on their surface through time. Briars wind their way upwards through the spaces between the stones, embracing them so future generations will love the land as much as those before them. A patina of moss attaches itself to the upper stones and covers them like altar linens in a well cared for church.

Events like bonfire night filled my leaving list of things to do. My cousin Mary and I could not attend because we were too young.

On this visit I begged to go, "Because this is my last chance. I am leaving Ireland." It worked.

It was Saint John's Eve and the summer solstice on June 23rd. The fire was lit at sunset and tended until the next morning. We danced and sang and ran wild through the night. The fire lit up the sky. The farmers said prayers for good crops and we felt the spirits and fairies all around us. It was magical.

A stone wall with a slit in it separated the Derradda house from the two room schoolhouse that my cousins attended in early years. I attended classes there to keep me occupied for two weeks until their school year was over and my cousins Mary and Timmy were set free. I felt like a celebrity. The teacher introduced me, "I'd like you to meet Maeve who has come all the way from the big city of Dublin," and inferred that I probably knew already what they were studying. I didn't. That June would be the last time I would attend Derradda School.

Mary and I thought up new adventures each day. One day after seeing my sister sitting on top of the barn roof with a friend, we decided to try it. We climbed the sidewall of the barn by stepping into spaces in the bricks and hoisted ourselves to the rooftop. We were enjoying our new vantage point when our grandmother caught sight of us on the roof.

"Get off there right now! What are ye doing?"

Two routes diverged upon a roof, and I took the one less traveled. My cousin, using better judgment, descended the way we came up. I went the opposite direction, jumped onto a lower roof and then another lower roof that happened to be the chicken house. I fell completely through the roof onto the chickens sitting contentedly inside. There was clucking and the flying of feathers but I landed on a nice bed of hay with stunned hens dashing out the door. Granny was so angry but mostly scared that we would do such a thing. That evening she went to the back of the house to pick a rod to let us have it when Aunt Mary and Uncle Paddy arrived. I took advantage of the situation, running to my aunt as she entered the door saying,

"Save us, save us."

She did. "They won't do it again," she said.

Timing is everything.

That last summer we went to the bog with my Uncle Willy and Aunt Mary from America. It was an adventure like no other. Aunt Mary emerged from her bedroom in the back of the house dressed like an American cowgirl. She sported a check shirt and wide pants with a straw hat secured beneath her chin.

"I can do that," she insisted as she took the reins of the donkey out of Willy's hands.

"Go ahead then. Sure, have ye a go at it."

"Surely, we'll end up in the ditch," my cousin whispered to me. The donkey let out a harsh braying sound, "eee-aaah,eeeaaah" and kicked the back of the cart. The white gloves Aunt Mary wore protected her delicate hands from the roughness of the reins. Off we went, holding on tight to the sides of the cart.

"Let her have her way now, let ye. Loosen a smidgeen on the reins."

The donkey was the happiest to finally arrive and Aunt Mary was triumphant.

The first job was to make a fridge in the bog by cutting into a bank of solid sod thus forming a space. Here we placed the milk and fresh baked bread for afternoon tea. We caught water from a stream in a tin can, boiled it and steeped the tealeaves until it turned black.

"Bog tea is so heavy," my uncle would say, "you could trot a mule on it."

The bog looked solid but it was 90% water and only 10% solid. The dark magic contained its own memories and life. It survives with its insect-trapping plants and green moss drenched in water while purple heather plants surround the edges. It holds secrets of the past in its wild landscape, devoid of oxygen and bacteria. It holds the history of Ireland. A body of a man was found from the early Bronze Age who lived about 4,000 years ago, with his skin still intact and arm reaching forward, mummified in place. For centuries hundreds of accounts of buried bog butter dug up by an unsuspecting farmer were published. An 18th century poem shows how common it was to find butter wrapped in leaves or carved wood containers:

But let his faith be good or bad,

He in his house great plenty had,

Of burnt oat-bread, and butter found,

With Garlik mixt, in boggy ground.

On that day I fell into the bog's blackness and felt the spongy warm wetness between my toes. My shoes slipped off. It was a great scary feeling! Mary pulled me out as we both laughed through the surprise of it all. Our Aunt Mary laughed so hard; tears ran down her face. The men were busy digging and cutting turf and did not see us. We rode home on top of the pile of turf in the donkey cart, our feet soaking wet. The light mist intensified the smell of woody moss and heather flowers that lined our path. We were glad Willy drove the heavy load back home though it wasn't as exciting as watching Aunt Mary.

Everything lived on, deep beneath its soggy surface. Perhaps the bog wanted to claim me when I slipped in, wanted me to stay.

I was released. My shoe sacrifice was accepted. Perhaps it had to do with outgrowing my well-worn shoes to face the painful transitions of childhood and embark on the journey that lay ahead.

The area had a small population of tinker camps with their brightly colored horse-drawn covered wagons parked on the side of the road. History is unclear about their origins but it is often explained that they are displaced farmers from the time of Oliver Cromwell. His massacre and ethnic cleansing of the Irish people forced many to leave their homes and settle in less fertile land in the West of Ireland.

'To hell or to Connaught" was the choice given then, and remembered today.

A knock on the door brought Granny running. The tinkers knew her as a generous woman who gave them any little job she could as well as a piece of bread and jam and a few potatoes.

"Pots to fix? I do grand work, ye know, for a few pence," they begged in a guttural heavy accent.

Sara Follon, the old woman of the roads, spoke only Gaelic. She survived going door-to-door by asking for a handful of sheep's wool that she gathered in a black bag slung over her shoulder, which she'd sell on market day. As children we would see her making her way up our path to the front door. She opened it and sat by the fire. This would send us scurrying for help, as we did not want to be alone with her. In addition to the wool, a piece of bread and butter, a cup of tea and the warmth of the fire was all she wanted.

We were told, "If you don't behave yourselves, Sara Follon will put you in her bag and take you away."

Whenever she arrived at the house, this threat created terror in our hearts. Her real story is not clear but I was told later that her family abandoned her for having a child out of wedlock. Judgment and guilt were harsh and defined her lonely life.

I don't know the exact moment when they appeared after I returned to Dublin, but two imaginary friends came into my life.

Perhaps they arrived because my two best real friends left Ireland, one for Canada and the other for South Africa. Perhaps because growing up was becoming complicated and moving to America was getting closer and closer. Dad left for America to set us up in an apartment. In came Susie and Tessie, regular girls and good friends. They lived separately in the atmosphere of my world, and if one was not home when I called, the other always was. They did not require any sleep but did everything else the same as I did. Fantasy and reality merged. We spoke about what was going on and they would let me know their thoughts and opinions. Small problems were discussed and solved. Susie was the most helpful in talking about going to America. Tessie didn't want anything to do with it.

"That's a stupid idea," she would say. "We have everything we need right here in Ireland."

Susie took an alternative position.

"Maeve, I saw a great book on America in Kavanagh's on George's Street. It's got loads of pictures and you could see exactly what New York looks like. Since we don't have any money, we could 'borrow it' and return it to the shelf when we are done. I'm coming to America with you, so I want to see too."

My subconscious soared, alternating the pro and con arguments about America and other challenges. I freely spoke about my imaginary friends to my family. Grainne told me directly that I was daft and to "be careful telling anyone about them." Mom took it in stride with her most impressive parental wisdom.

Piano lessons were part of my extra school schedule, given once a week in a small room with a very large piano by a not-so-inspiring and sadistic nun. The lessons were practiced at home by spreading out a long piece of white paper, resembling actual piano keys on the dining room table. We did not own a piano. As insane as this sounds, I brought it to another level of disbelief.

"Mom, Tessie is also studying the piano and needs to practice. Can she take a turn?"

We both sat and listened to the silence while Tessie took her seat and practiced her lesson. I smiled and moved my head in accompaniment. There was less time for me to have to play the imaginary piano. It goes without saying that Mom was totally brilliant by not smashing my need to entertain imaginary friends. I can only think she must have been howling inside but I never knew it. One day when I could not successfully reproduce the assigned piano lesson at school, the nun took up a chair to throw it at me. I ran out the door and never returned. This was one of those defining moments when I decided what was right and acted to exercise my own will. Tessie stopped taking piano lessons around the same time. We told no one. The paper piano keys did not reveal our lack of progress.

My imaginary friends and I had our own language. "Indepotable" was our favorite word for anything or anyone we did not like. Indepotable food is totally unacceptable and we cannot eat it. The indepotable boy who bullied everyone as they walked by his house and the indepotable flowered dress that was bought for me to wear, were examples of its use.

One fine day I went too far, too many times. Mom discovered a Waterford glass that had been smashed and confronted me about doing it.

"Ah, I did not do it. Susie broke it," I said.

Mom took a second to collect herself and replied, "Well from now on, the next time Susie breaks something, I am going to hold you responsible."

The gig was up, I knew. For a good while though I tested friendship and the limits of my behavior through my two best imaginary friends.

The extreme Catholic world within which I grew up opened my imagination to fantastic storytelling, to suspending belief in the rational and being quite comfortable with the irrational and invisible. So much of religion is based on blind faith, accepting what is not known and seen, a faith built on mysteries. The real world lacked that excitement.

Catholicism did an excellent job of creating uncertainty about my very existence. From a young age I knew about the transitory nature of life on earth. Purgatory existed for those not pure enough to enter heaven. It was to my benefit to stay on good terms with God. My bedtime prayer, said while kneeling by the side of my bed before I was tucked in was written in the 18th century. It went like this:

Now I lay me down to sleep.

I pray the Lord my soul to keep.

And if I die before I wake,

I pray to God my soul to take.

Not exactly the most calming way to lay your head on the pillow and go to sleep. Do you really want to think of your own demise each night when the lights go out?

Another more comforting prayer, which is really the first stanza of the "If I die before I wake" prayer, surrounded me with spirits and charms of the unknown. Four men stared at me the entire night for my protection.

There are four corners on my bed

There are four angels at each head.

Matthew, Mark, Luke and John

God bless me and the bed I lay on.

My time was running out for 'last things.' So many thoughts rushed through my young mind; I couldn't keep up with them. Nothing comforted me. I would leave the land of my birth.

Chapter 5

And so the leaving day arrived in August of 1958 and I opened my eyes from a restless sleep to my very last day in Ireland. Mom, Grainne and I were taking the train from Dublin to Cobh in County Cork to board the Cunard Line ship, the Britannic, for our trip to New York City. Goodbyes were everywhere with the adjoining remark,

"When you come back to visit Ireland, you'll be real Yanks."

Grainne was very excited about going to America. For her it was a dream come true, having listened to so many conversations at the dinner table about how great America was. Our Aunt Mary already lived in New York and would send us packages of the latest American dresses and Wrigley's chewing gum. We loved her visits to Derradda and Dublin. Two to three large bags of the most fashionable of clothes came with her and guaranteed a striking new look every day. The Christmas before we left, Dad sent me a teenage doll with nylon stockings and high-heeled shoes. She was quite the novelty. I took her everywhere and never unscrewed her head. Dad sent high school books on American History and English texts to familiarize Grainne with the American way of learning. She studied with Sister Dymphna to prepare for the enormous change in her early teenage years.

"I can't believe we are actually going to New York. I'm so happy," she would exclaim.

In so many ways she was Americanized while still in Ireland. With four years separating us, she comprehended the opportunities of our soon-to-be new world better than I.

The train rocked back and forth making its way through the misty green fields, as though resisting its own forward motion to our port of departure. It whizzed past the countryside as the cows raised their heavy heads to witness the unwanted intrusion, and the sheep ran in all directions, not knowing the particular demands the approaching train whistles were making. I wondered if there were sheep in New York.

Known for being the last port of call for the Titanic in 1912, Cobh was a storybook town with its bright yellow, turquoise and red row houses proudly facing the Atlantic Ocean. Blue and green small fishing boats bobbed in the harbor as we approached our hotel by taxi: a town so deceptively serene. A woman greeted us in the hotel lobby. She was "the breadth of Balla and half Manulla," as my Uncle Willy would say. The streets in the Irish towns of Balla and Manulla are very wide. She then said with a big smile on her face as she bent all the way down to meet me at eye level,

"So yer going to America, are ye? Isn't that grand?"

You stupid old lady. Do I look happy to you? Sure, we came all the way from Dublin just to see other poor people leave Ireland. Yes we're going, and it's not grand at all!

Cobh was the gateway to the New World for emigrants both willing and unwilling. It was the first stop for Queen Victoria on her initial visit to Ireland in 1829 and she re-named it Queensland, after herself. It reverted in 1921 to its real, Gaelic name, Cobh. There is a "next year in Jerusalem" aspect to Cobh. The exodus from Ireland caused by the Great Potato Famine in 1845 continued for many years, spreading Irish men and women across the globe. It was from this port that most of the 'Irish convicts' in the dreaded coffin ships sailed to

Australia, barely surviving the trip. Many of the so-called hardened criminals were women and children and patriots for a free Ireland. Cobh Cemetery sadly is also remembered as the burial place for those bodies plucked from the sea when the Lusitania was torpedoed by Germany. This lovely harbor witnessed so much hope and anguish through time.

We stayed at the Bellavista Lodging House down the street from St. Coleman's Cathedral. Any picture of Cobh shows the gigantic neo-Gothic Cathedral perched on a hill overseeing the entire town and harbor. In 1916 the Bellavista became the Sacred Heart Novitiate for the Sisters of Mercy until they left in the 1930s. Their spirits remained. The hallway still displayed a picture of the entranceway where a group of young nuns stood looking serious and pious in their white novice habits. I couldn't sleep that night but instead listened to the rattling of the rosary beads worn by those walking in the hallway just outside my door. Whispers of repetitious short prayers or ejaculations wafted into our room.

"Jesus, Mary and Joseph save us" and "Mary, Star of the Sea, protect us."

In the salty harbor breeze the decaying iron chains holding smaller ships to the concrete dock clanked away in the night.

The carillon bells of the cathedral struck each hour and rang out for early Mass the morning of our departure.

That morning Grainne and I saw Mom's nervousness as she prepared to leave. She was all for going to America but was terrified of the four-day trip across the Atlantic and becoming seasick. We tendered out to the ship with fear all around. We were pulled onto the ship by sailors who reached for us as the boats splashed and hit against each other.

"Grab my arm," they shouted and we were pulled on board.

We stood on the deck as the Britannic slowly left the harbor, and watched the bright colors of the row houses shrink to mere dots upon the shore. My Aunt Eve who arrived to give Mom support waved and cried as we left.

"Goodbye. Come back to visit us soon."

She was my godmother. I never saw her again.

Being on a trans-Atlantic ship with the opulence and art was surreal. It provided the best distraction for this major life change as it magically floated a city of people through the waves, dragging the whole Atlantic Ocean behind it. The Grand Dining Hall was three stories high and we held our breath as we descended the spiral staircase grasping onto the richly carved oak bannisters. Grainne's mouth was wide open when I turned to see her and get validation that all this was real.

"Magic…" I whispered to Grainne. "It doesn't look real…"

The walls were decorated with large traditional murals depicting lounging women and men, drinking and feasting in pastoral scenes. In the center of the dining room there was a ten-foot globe of the world underneath a ceiling of lights. We were escorted to table 18 that we shared with a Jewish family consisting of parents and two teenage sons returning from a holiday in Ireland.

Facing me at the table was a fabric tapestry of a white unicorn lying peacefully in a field of small flowers, surrounded by a fence low enough to jump over if it wanted to. It immediately captured my imagination.

"What is that animal in the picture?" I whispered to Grainne.

"It's a unicorn and it's not real. It's a fairy-tale animal," she answered like a true older sister.

"Well, how do you know it's not real? " I asked. "I like it very much." It was clear I was comfortable identifying with a mythical creature that was different by nature and gratified by its own differentness. I felt bewitched.

The unicorn was an other-worldly spiritual being, with hidden powers to attract and survive, and so I attached my mind to this image to soften the enormous feeling of being overwhelmed by everything that was happening in my life. I was powerless, fenced in like the unicorn, except like it, I could jump over the fence, if only in my mind. My attention returned to the white tablecloths and perfect white napkins propped on plates. Individual cups of butter rolled into little balls waited at each setting. The red-jacketed waiter bowed as he placed the napkin on my lap and a small green salad on my plate. He gave me a big smile.

Everything is going to be great. If America is anything like this boat, it may not be so bad after all.

Grainne had the strongest constitution for the trip, so she went to the pool each day with the boys from the table. Mammy and I were both sea sick. Bridget's stomach notified her that the scrumptious breakfast she just completed, wanted to leave the premises. Now.

"What's wrong?" I asked as she covered her mouth with her napkin and jumped from the table. The mother of the boys, Grainne and I ran with her. She made it to the railing.

I've never seen her sick like this. Will she die? I don't feel so good myself.

Mammy and I stayed in the cabin for the rest of the day.

"Come, let's walk on the deck together to clear our heads," she said in the evening, and we walked and walked the whole perimeter of the ship, steadying ourselves by holding on to each other.

On the second day the three of us looked out on the water on the way to lunch and there was not a wave in sight. It was on that day that we heard of ice ahead and the captain slowed the boat's speed as we navigated through it. Mom stopped in front of the lifeboats stacked on the side of the ship, staring at them as though she was counting and calculating if there would be enough for all the people on board. Enough for the three of us. She was terrified of another Titanic catastrophe.

On the morning of our arrival, everyone on the boat rushed to the starboard side of the ship to see what was called the Statue of Liberty. I couldn't understand why everyone was so excited. Children were being held up on shoulders, an old man was crying and people were calling out,

"There she is, there she is!" It was as though a real person was standing out in the New York harbor welcoming us to America.

This must be why we came clear across the Atlantic Ocean.., why we left Ireland.

Though I didn't completely understand the full meaning, I internalized that feeling of joy and celebration. It wasn't until my mid-sixties when I re-visited the Statue that unexpectedly the emotions I witnessed as a child surfaced within me. Upon seeing the statue and reading the quote from Emma Lazarus' sonnet, *The New Colossus*, I was moved to tears.

Not like the brazen giant of Greek fame,
With conquering limbs astride from land to land;
Here at our sea-washed, sunset gates shall stand
A mighty woman with a torch, whose flame
Is the imprisoned lightning, and her name
Mother of Exiles. From her beacon-hand
Glows world-wide welcome; her mild eyes command
The air-bridged harbor that twin cities frame.

"Keep, ancient lands, your storied pomp!" cries she
With silent lips.

"Give me your tired, your poor,
Your huddled masses yearning to breathe free,
The wretched refuse of your teeming shore.
Send these, the homeless, tempest-tossed to me,
I lift my lamp beside the golden door!"

We docked at Pier 90 on the Upper West Side to bravely face our unknown and frightening new world. I knew now we would be safe, once I was in Daddy's arms, even if we weren't in Ireland.

Chapter 6

As told to Maeve...

Bridget's feet touched the pavement of New York a second time. A surge of past memories surfaced about New York City when she had arrived there in 1926. Bridget's Aunt Marie Ray and her husband Charles owned a flourishing hat business that catered to the Broadway theatre crowd. She recalled an image of where she lived on West 26th street near Broadway, a long way from Derradda in the West of Ireland. It was a charming brownstone building with a beckoning stoop, tall windows and metal ceilings. As a single young woman she was taking on America by herself. Not just America; Bridget was entering the world of the upper echelon of New York City.

In contrast, the traditional daughter's role in the farming family was the hardest one by far. Her prospects of ever inheriting the farm in agricultural Ireland were few and far between. Bridget's brother Willy would inherit the Derradda farm, as was the custom. Destiny determined that her choices were emigration, enter a convent or marry a wonderful farmer. The socialization process of a daughter instilled a sense of subordination to the rest of the family. The Meehan family of Derradda never forgot the importance of protecting the future interests of their daughters, while still guaranteeing the inheritance rights of their sons. Bridget completed secretarial school in Westport, Co. Mayo the year before coming to America with the plan of emigrating and building a career.

Traveling to America was part of family history. Bridget's mother had traveled to Cleveland where many friends and family made their home. Granny chose to return to Ireland and to the farm in Derradda.

Bridget recalled her initial overwhelming reaction to the hustle and bustle of New York City: the buildings piled on top of one another like competing mountains; the smell of the city heat that took her breath away. Most of all, she recalled her determination to succeed as a professional woman. She was, despite her inner sophistication, a young Irish Catholic girl, "just off the boat."

At the young age of ten, I had no understanding of her life as a young woman in New York City, so many years ago. She understood the challenges my sister and I would be facing and hoped she and Dad had made the right decision to return to America.

The hat business was a thriving international industry during the 1920s and '30s. Hats were the most important accessories that either enhanced or destroyed a person's image. Bridget learned that the kind of headgear people chose, defined how they saw themselves and how they fit into American and European culture.

Charlie Ray loved the process of hat making. He was a master at it and enjoyed sharing his talent with his smart niece. She advanced from *la nouvelle* (the new girl) to *apprentice en chef,* or head apprentice within a year. Hats were designed by the milliners of the day by using hat blocks made from wood, carved to form a particular style. The technique of blocking or shaping felt or straw on wood forms created the hat design. Sculpting the material was an art, using steam and hot irons. The hats were then placed in a drying cupboard followed by applying a stiffening material that was, in itself, a delicate process. Trimming was the finishing touch. Marie had a knack for designing entirely unconventional looks loved by the theatre crowd. Bridget was in Central Park one Sunday afternoon and came upon geese feathers around a pond. The geese were molting.

"Aunt Marie, look what I found today for you!"

They ended up on Madame Ray's hats the next month.

Hat styles followed the changes that were occurring with women's enlightenment and independence. They mirrored the social and political changes in all their different styles. The designers like Madame Ray were on the cutting edge of those changes in their workrooms and their lives. The cloche was one such design that followed the fashion of short hair for women with tightly fitting, helmet-like hats that fit snugly over the ears, tilted to one side. The wearer pulled the hat over her forehead and looked down her nose to see. It created an effect that said,

"I am the new woman of the '20s. A modern woman with bold new ideas."

Madame Ray re-introduced the turban hat style which was cloth wrapped horizontally around a mold and accessorized with feathers and jewels. It was used especially for eveningwear.

Marie amplified notions of gutsiness and ambition. She left the West of Ireland with a girlfriend and together they made their way to Cleveland where they worked as seamstresses. San Francisco was their next stop. In 1906 they were staying in a wooden Victorian house in Nob Hill when they were thrown out of their beds at 5:15 in the morning. They experienced what was one of the greatest natural disasters in history, the San Francisco earthquake. The city burned for three days and over 3,000 people died. A stench of burning buildings and human flesh filled the streets. The survivors slept in tents in parks and the city required people to cook outside in order to limit the possibility of new fires. The U.S. Army intervened, providing food and clothing to the refugee camps. The house where Marie lived was dynamited after the fires in the area destroyed many of the buildings. Marie, in later years, spoke about how strangely calm everyone was in the streets and camps, despite the disaster and personal loss.

Fairy tale or not, along came her knight in shining armor, Charles Ray, who rescued both women. He took them to his own house where he lived with his mother in an area that was not affected by the earthquake or fires. The romance that lasted a lifetime began. They stayed in San Francisco for about ten years and then moved to New York City.

When Marie and Charlie visited Derradda, everyone was thrilled to see them. They stayed at the Mulranny Hotel and drove up the boreen in their fancy car. She never forgot her roots but America was now her home. Heads turned when they appeared on a scene. Everyone took notice. He was over six feet, slim and swanky looking in striped suits that only accentuated his height. She was beautiful in her fashionable furs, elegant dresses, long leather gloves up to her elbows, and stylish hats.

Marie went to the Wall Street trading floor every week and made them millionaires. She simply had a knack for it. One day she returned home very quickly.

"Why are you back so fast?" Charlie asked.

"A black cat darted out from the JP Morgan Bank. He stopped short when he saw me and gave the loudest meow. Then he darted around the corner. I'm not trading today. Bad luck," she answered. Enterprising, elegant and superstitious.

He referred to her as "my great kid" even though she was older than he was by a couple of years. He was mad about her. Charlie was of Danish descent and Bridget thought that was the reason he took a long time to warm up to people. The opposite side of his personality showed when he had a drink of Danish vodka. Quickly inebriated, he became comical and talkative.

The Ford Industrial Exposition held in New York City in 1928 attracted over a million people along with the Rays and Bridget. A new four-door Model A with leather seats replaced the well know Model T car. As soon as it was released at the end of the year, they owned one in classic green with black leather seats and a radio as an accessory. It had a top speed of 65 miles per hour, unheard of in previous models. Bridget could not help but feel she had time-traveled herself into the future on the Model A's first run in NYC. Marie drove at full speed up Broadway. It felt like she was flying as the silver quail ornament on the hood of the car flapped its wings as it flew through the city streets. Styles were changing. Views of women were changing. Bridget's mood was one of exuberance and excitement.

"That's the fastest I've ever moved! Weren't you afraid of running over someone or crashing into a car coming the other way?" Bridget asked.

"That's the thrill of it, Bridget. Knowing you can control the car. Feeling your own independence. It's the future right in your own hands."

Milliners set the tone for fashion on both sides of the Atlantic with the most famous in Paris, Milan, Vienna and New York. Couture houses were established headed by the premier designers, all of whom demanded to be addressed as "Madame." Marie Ray was no exception. Hers was a name well-known in New York fashion circles though not on the international scene. Marie was also savvy enough to know that when certain prestigious clients came to her store and wanted to meet her in person, she would have her second in command say, "Oh I am so sorry but Madame Ray is in Paris for a week introducing her latest creation." There were those who would not buy hats from someone Irish.

Lily Dache, a French-trained milliner who settled in New York City, was the most famous milliner in the United States. It was her influence that initially paved the way for Marie to be able to develop her talents and creativity in hat design. She was generous in her willingness to collaborate with other professionals and the two women enjoyed the social scene together along with their husbands. Lily's clients included stars like Carmen Miranda and Marlene Dietrich. Her unique creations included what was called chic toques, a hat with a narrow or no brim and demure cloth snoods, designed to hold the hair in place over the back of the head.

Bridget accompanied Charles and Marie to Sardi's one night during the holiday season in December and it was here she first met Lily Dache. She was as famous in the restaurant as the celebrities whose pictures lined the walls. Lily burst into the room. Long black feathers on a three-cornered red satin hat lifted her in the air, as on a gust of wind, past the other diners to the corner table where they were seated.

Bridget was just about to taste her first Oyster Rockefeller, but quickly replaced it on the plate. Marie believed oysters of all kinds should slide down your throat on a weekly basis as they were one of the healthiest foods you could eat. Marie and Lily kissed European style and then, after squeezing herself into a space beside Bridget, kissed her exclaiming how delighted she was to meet her and, "Welcome to New York, my dear." Lily chatted business about a new client in the theatre district and Marie told her of a hat design she created using peacock feathers and purple felt.

As she was leaving to join her party of friends, Lily said to Bridget, "My dear, glamour is what makes a man ask for your telephone number, but it also is what makes a woman ask for the name of your milliner."

Bridget smiled at such a colorful character giving her advice but responded with the deference called for in the moment, "Of course, Madame. Thank you for that."

Bridget's transformation was occurring at a rapid pace in the competent hands of Madame Ray. Part of her modernization was to get her hair cut in a "bob" style of the day. Many times Bridget told the story of the Irish cop on the corner of 26th Street who greeted her as she passed by each day.

Noticing her hairstyle change, he remarked with a lilting voice, "It didn't take too long for them to cut your hair, now did it?" Bridget blushed.

"Well, I must be in style in America. Isn't that right?"

Life changed when the stock market crashed in October of 1929. It marked the end of the "Roaring Twenties." The bubble of prosperity burst and along with it the very foundations of the American dream were shredded. The Rays lost almost all their money and the hat business began to lose customers. When the shop had to be closed, Bridget was able to secure a job at the Cattle Club with her secretarial education. It was she who supported the Rays for a brief period of time until they were able to slowly recover. The dairy industry in the United States was big business at the time. The tracking and registration of all breeds was necessary as buying and selling from the ranches in the southern to the northern states increased. This was not the glamorous job Bridget anticipated she would be doing, but she had a good job in hard times.

The American Jersey Cattle Club, located at 324 West 23rd Street in N.Y.C. had a definite masculine feel to it. Dark leather couches and chairs with heavy arms were arranged around the reception area, with large framed pictures of cows on the walls staring blankly back at their brokers. To the right sat a secretarial pool of men and women adjoining the reception area where visitors were readily seen and greeted. The cows actually comforted Bridget as she would look up from her desk and see them eyeing her. They reminded her of the cows in the fields of Derradda, staring and blinking, waiting to come home to be milked in the evening. Books detailing types of breeds and characteristics sat on the small inlaid leather tabletops for light reading while customers waited to be seen.

John Porter owned a thriving cattle ranch in southern Texas. He arrived one day to meet with the president of the company. He was tall and good looking, confident in his manner and striking in appearance. He wore a beige linen suit with brown cowboy boots and of course a large broad rimmed cowboy hat. Bridget wondered, given the outfit, where he left his horse on 23rd Street. He looked like the quintessential American. As Bridget escorted him to the office in the back, he took an immediate liking to her.

John pulled her aside following his meeting and asked in his Texas drawl, "I'd be honored if you would accompany me to a gala dinner this weekend at the Waldorf Astoria. I'm here in New York for business and having a beautiful lady like you on my arm, why, I'd be the envy of the evening."

Before she knew what she was saying, she said, "I would love to."

It followed after many months of roses, perfume and Belgian chocolates that John wanted her to move to Texas with him. He was in love. She was not. She explained in later years, that he was the kind of man that "always got what he wanted," but for her there was something indefinable missing. The Southern charm was not enough.

Her best friend, Noreen, from Dublin said, "Well you can grow to love him. What are you doing throwing him back with all that money? I'll take him for sure."

Noreen was obsessed with marrying a wealthy American. A few years later the entire company moved to Texas with John as CEO and the offices in New York closed.

My father, Jim Walsh came to New York as a young man about a year after Bridget to live with relatives in Woodhaven, Queens. Before he left Castlebar in Co Mayo, he was outfitted in a new Irish tweed suit for America. Shortly after his arrival he was quickly told that it was not the "right cut" to make it in New York. The lapels were wrong, the sleeves not wide enough and the pants did not have a cuff. Jimmy's uncle, Peter Brady, owned a speak-easy on 63rd Street and Lexington Avenue called Brady's, right across from the Barbizon Hotel. It was a perfect place for Jim to start bar tending during Prohibition and learn about New York culture at the same time. The two instinctively liked each other and Peter knew Jim would be a star in the business. People from all classes, races and walks of life socialized, drank together and listened to jazz. The Barbizon Hotel, which opened in 1927, was a club residence for professional single women, many of whom were in the theatre or the arts. Men were not allowed above the first floor in its early years. The women walked across the street, met their favorite daddy and drank liquor from teacups in the back room, to disguise that they were drinking booze. The back room was accessible from a hallway in the back of the restaurant. Floor to ceiling bookshelves stacked with discarded dusty law books disguised the entrance to the room. Peter had been studying law for a few years but the money to be made during prohibition demanded all his time. Inside it was deliberately dark with flickering candles on the small round tables that seated two to four people. The furniture was well used. The red velvet couch showed visible wear and tear. The oak bar was the length of the room at the far end, with most of the bottles underneath the counter and out of sight.

Peter purchased an original music box to fill the back room with ragtime tunes from musical artists of the day. The Regina Music Box Company sales room located on 22nd Street and Broadway was known as America's finest music box maker. Jim and he visited often to marvel at the latest precursor to the modern jukebox. Large revolving metal discs with holes that plucked the tuned teeth of a steel comb produced the music. Peter finally purchased one for $50.00. He believed that music made the drinks taste better, the time disappear and the company more convivial.

A back door opened onto an alleyway that led to 63rd Street for an easy exit should the need arise. Though it was a known juice joint, it was never raided. The cops frequented the illegal establishment.

Jimmy made a martini and an old fashioned like no one else. The ultra-orthodox, soon-to-be Archbishop slipped into the speak-easy on a weekly basis. He liked to convince the parishioners he met there that he was only performing his pastoral duties.

"What will you have tonight, Your Excellency?" Jim asked.

"Leave the Excellency off, Jimmy. I'm trying to blend in with the common man. I was home in my study writing the homily for Sunday's Mass on the temptations of the flesh and got an urge for one of your glasses of fine Irish whiskey. Jameson. Straight up, as usual."

Jimmy was a star, as was the Archbishop, with the women from the Barbizon who would come in groups to socialize and drink wearing their short hair and knee length flapper dresses. Some came wearing pants. They would line up at the bar, asking for their favorite bartender.

"Where's Jimmy?" they would yell through their perfectly painted crimson lips.

"He makes the best cocktail on the Upper East Side."

Prohibition opened the doors for women to drink alongside the men in bars and not just at the tables in restaurants. The new independent woman was out on her own, not wearing a corset, listening to jazz and enjoying herself. The behavior was lamented by some as a sure sign of society's moral decline. As times do change, the new styles were accepted and a more relaxed and democratic way of dressing and behaving won the day.

Jimmy shared another world with some of the ladies of the Barbizon. He attended acting school at the New York School for Dramatic Arts. It was his love. The realities of life prevented him from continuing. He had a talent for the spoken word. A new customer, after listening to him speak one night at the crowded bar, remarked, "You speak English good." He replied with a dead-on look and wry smile, "Yes. I speak English well." Later World War II and supporting a family made acting an impossible dream.

Prohibition was a failed experiment. Booze cruises, Blind Pigs and creative cocktails triumphed. When prohibition was repealed in 1930, President Roosevelt said, "What America needs now is a drink."

On a summer evening in 1931, two young kindred spirits, separate in their lives, similar in their dreams, were joined by fate. They grew up in towns next door to each other in the West of Ireland, yet met one Saturday night at the United Irish Counties Association dinner and dance in New York City. This was a place to touch base with the familiar, with being Irish, with home. It was an easy place to relax at the end of the week. Jim spotted Bridget across the room in the middle of a group of friends from the Cattle Club. She immediately knew he was coming her way to ask her to dance the new American dance, the Lindy Hop, that she had just learned last week. She stood out in the crowd wearing the latest dress fashion for women that she had made herself; a red and white floral, high-waisted dress that sloped at her neck and stopped just below her knees, with a wide white belt and flared skirt perfect for dancing. He was dapper looking with his best American suit on, wide black and white geometric tie, black-cuffed pants and winning smile.

"I would be honored to have this dance," he said.

Within seconds they were in sync on the dance floor, moving back and forth, swinging out and then returning, all the time holding hands, as though they had danced together for years. From that dance on, they were in step on and off the dance floor. They were married at Holy Trinity Catholic Church on West 82nd Street in Manhattan in a simple ceremony in May, 1933. The Byzantine Church, built of brick and terra cotta, is adorned with multicolored mosaics and patterned tiles, as well as marble and gold leaf. The dome glistening with Guastavino ceiling tiles ascends 100 feet into the air above the marble floor tiles imported from Florence, Italy. They pledged their love forever in this brilliantly designed interior. It was a glorious space befitting their union.

Gerard was born ten months later in 1934 in New York City. Mom took a trip home to Ireland with Gerard just before World War II began in September of 1939. Dad stayed in New York. She could not return to America because of travel restrictions during the war. Frightening and lonely years followed.

Mom and Gerard lived with my godmother, Evelyn, outside of Dublin. As they sat around the table in the back kitchen one day, the back door opened slowly and a man's hat came flying in. It landed on the floor at Bridget's feet. Gerard jumped to defend his mother.

"Who's there?" he yelled.

Dad opened the door wide with the biggest of smiles and ran to hug both of them.

"How did you get here?" What happened? Oh, Jim. I can't believe it."

Dad was fortunate to be one of the many civilians conscripted by the Lockheed Airforce Base in September, 1943, located in Northern Ireland to join the war effort for building and repairing planes.

The letter read, "Mr. James Walsh, at the request of the United States Military Authorities… traveling under orders… is authorized to travel by air and is qualified to carry certain classified documents." He didn't know where he was going until told on the plane on route to Northern Ireland. He drove immediately to Dublin on a two-day leave.

Bridget accompanied Jim back to Northern Ireland. Gerard went to live with his grandmother in the West of Ireland to avoid the reality of war in that part of Great Britain.

"I want to go with you. Don't leave me here."

"You'll be safe here," Dad told him. "We'll be back to get you as soon as the war is over."

The fog of war finally ended. Separation and sadness were etched upon their lives again.

But their dreams were given a second chance by returning to America in 1958. Dad stood out on the pier, dressed to impress American style, wearing a red and white striped tie and white button down collar shirt. Tears streamed down his face as he spotted us. We ran to him at the same time.

Chapter 7

Grainne and I stepped onto New York City streets in August of 1958 carrying within us our family history of adventure. Major transformations awaited. Immigration itself was the first.

I speak of transformation in terms of consciousness. I do not mean obvious life changes: growing from childhood to adulthood and old age, career, marriage, pregnancy and divorce or illness and recovery. By consciousness I mean undergoing profound changes in beliefs and breaking with the past.

The first transformation of becoming an American was thrust upon me. Leaving the familiar, what I loved, what I knew, to forge a new identity was overwhelming. I was a child and as such, powerless in the face of adult decisions. Feelings of loss, fear, mistrust, acceptance, rejection and anger all tumbled deep within me.

We met relatives I had never seen. The Brady's were from Dad's side of the family. "Welcome to New York," they said with big smiles and hugs. Aunty Mary and Uncle Paddy were there from Mom's side. I knew them.

Grainne and I were suddenly in the back seat of Dad's 1956 black, four-door Dodge Coronet. I sat by the window and became very quiet as I watched New York City unfold. We headed for the 59th Street Bridge on our way to Woodside, Queens. I closed the window to escape the suffocating humid air from rushing in. I couldn't breathe. I was trapped. Tall gray walls concealed the sky. Horns honked. Piles of garbage simmered on the sidewalks. It smelled like vomit. People darted between cars. Trains rattled above our heads. I sank further down in the seat. The car took us deeper and deeper into where we would be living. My parents were happy and excited. I was scared. Grainne had her window open as she delighted in the brightly colored cars of the '50s.

"There's an orange one," she yelled. A minute later, "Look, a green and white one with wings."

The most disturbing sight was the large apartment buildings with metal stairs running down the outside. Laundry hung out to dry in the August sunlight. In Ireland, buildings that looked like this were in the very poor sections of Dublin, and so my first impression was that New York was one big slum. Already, I hated it.

Our new home was a two family house on 64th Street. We had the upstairs and an Italian older woman and her husband lived downstairs. She wanted her sister to get the apartment and created an unbearable time for my parents. We were a quiet family but she banged on the ceiling at all hours and shut the water off in the basement. I remember Mom crying and Dad trying to talk to our unfriendly neighbor, to no avail. Mom was afraid and so within a year we moved to a nicer and calmer apartment. The blending of ethnicities in the melting pot of America hadn't made it to our neighborhood.

Assimilation was the term used to describe how new immigrants became part of American society. Leave the past behind and become part of a diversified society, a mix of equal citizens within a new nation that offered limitless possibilities. Being Irish was what I knew, what I loved, and would never change. Becoming an American was the goal. It was not my desire to become an un-hyphenated American (American without "Irish" attached) and lose my Irish identity. I came face to face with these stereotypes of the Irish held by Americans of other ethnic groups and even Americans of Irish heritage. Most of these I found alien and insulting.

"Do the children wear shoes in Ireland?"

"Do you have Christmas trees in Ireland?"

"You must have lots of sisters and brothers."

"Ireland is part of Great Britain, isn't it?"

"Are you shanty Irish or lace curtain Irish?"

I recall those people with cynical smiles plastered over their all-knowing faces as they spoke of things they knew nothing about. My parents were acutely aware of these stereotypes.

Respectability and achievement became a strong part of our upbringing. Jim and Bridget raised their children in America and never lost their love of Ireland or the seeds of Irishness. They nurtured within themselves and each of their children, whether they realized it or not: humor, creativity, ancient loyalties, spirituality and a touch of rebelliousness.

My sister started at Saint Jean Baptiste High School in the Upper East Side of New York City at fourteen. She was shown once how to ride the subway from Woodside, Queens to the American high school in a largely French-oriented Catholic system. It was difficult adapting to American culture, a French high school run by the Sisters of Notre Dame, puberty, and the New York City Subway System all at the same time.

I attended the neighborhood Catholic elementary school, Saint Sebastian's, run by the Sisters of Charity. It was decided "it would not do me any harm" to be left back a year since there was no room in the fifth grade in the over-crowded parochial school. Public school was not an option. They had risked enough bringing us to America. In retrospect, it softened my transition since I knew most of the work. I just needed to mentally translate subjects from Gaelic back to English since I had learned many through Gaelic.

I felt alienated in unfamiliar routines. The first day of school I was shocked when everyone jumped to attention at the side of their desks to recite The Pledge of Allegiance.

"I pledge allegiance to the flag, of the United States of America . . ." with their hands across their chests and attention focused on the American flag at the front of the room.

What is happening?

Then we had atomic bomb drills. The bells sounded and we hid underneath our little wooden desks until all was clear. I never could figure out how those desks were going to protect us. This was not necessary in Ireland. I recall the day when I pronounced the letter 'Z' as 'Zed', which is how it is pronounced in Ireland. The class roared laughing and the nun asked me to repeat what I said. I was confused and embarrassed.

X, Y, Zed,

Sugar on my bread.

Tea in the morning

And cocoa going to bed

That's how I learned it. She told me how it was pronounced in America. "Zee."

I was not interested in making new friends, or altering my pronunciation of 'Z'. This worried Mom and Dad for a short time and then I suddenly snapped out of it. One day we were required to perform in front of the class, all forty of us. I had a talent for recitation with a little drama mixed in, and decided to recite a poem I learned in Elocution Class in Ireland. I fixed their eighty eyes with mine and gave the performance of my young lifetime.

The poem I chose was called *The Witch*. "*The witch, the witch that lived in the woods, is not very pretty and not very good. She has a long nose . . . and a cat that sits on her back.*"

I recited it in an eerie voice with gestures and scared some of the kids in the class. It was a big success, followed by the clapping of little hands. Quickly I found myself sent from classroom to classroom to perform with the same winning results. Somehow this broke through my self-imposed alienation and I returned to my adventurous self.

I was not at all prepared for the arrangement that Mom's cousin from Ireland, John, would be living with us. He was a huge man and a confirmed bachelor; quiet, happy to listen to his radio, read and take long walks. His bedroom was his world at nighttime. He surrounded himself with history, art and beauty at the Frick Museum in New York City where he worked as a security guard in the daytime. Surprisingly, Uncle John and I became fast friends. One day he took me to the Frick Museum for a personal tour. We walked among the great masters of European art. John pointed out the eyes of one that followed me around the room and the mouth of another that whispered, "Come closer and listen to what I have to say."

I was glued to her mouth when we were interrupted by two women asking, "Where are the Vermeer paintings? We're lost among all the pictures."

John had to nudge me along as we walked beneath floor to ceiling portraits, richly carved and upholstered armchairs that you were not allowed to sit on and bronze sculptures of naked nymphs. We arrived at pictures of a young girl laughing and another having a music lesson.

I thought of my unicorn from the dining room of the boat coming to America.

"John, do you have a picture of a unicorn here?" I asked, hoping they did.

"No, but I do know a place in New York where they do.

We can go on my next day off."

It seemed we traveled on the subway for days to reach the Cloisters in Upper Manhattan. John did not drive. There was my exact unicorn hung high on a wall all by itself, sitting in a circular fence. There were others but none as lovely as this one. John bought me a print of it and I hung it in my bedroom.

He knew about a lot of things, including algebra and geometry. I delivered math problems to his door. He figured out the right answer in a very convoluted way.

"Maeve, can you explain to the class how you reached the correct answer? Come to the chalkboard, please."

I did and diagramed it as John had written, but couldn't explain how I actually figured it out. The teacher either knew someone at home was very smart or thought I was a savant. Most likely she concluded the former. John and I had a special bond that lasted until he died in his sleep as quietly as he lived, one night late in life.

Then came the time to become a naturalized citizen of the United States. Because our parents were naturalized citizens, my sister and I could become naturalized through the process of derivation. Dad made an appointment for Grainne and I to meet with a judge in New York City. His chambers smelled old and moldy. A whiff of a smoldering pipe on the desk triggered a sweet memory of Uncle Willy puffing by the fire in Derradda.

We stood in his chambers and he asked me, "Do you want to become an American citizen?"

I replied, "No."

Dad gave me a kick in the shins and said, "She doesn't mean that. She wants to become a citizen."

The judge smiled at me, waited, and as I looked at Dad's panicked face, I said, "Yes."

He then asked a few more questions, one of which was "Will you bear arms for your country?"

I guess it was nervousness but I didn't think of myself going to war. I thought of having bare arms and started to giggle. We got through it. Grainne was a perfect adult. I was assured that we would have joint citizenship and be able to keep our Irish citizenship as well as become American.

It was in history class that America was revealed to me as a place I could call home. I read about the American Revolution, immigrants coming to find religious and political freedom, defying British rule and establishing a new Republic. I saw the similarity between the American fight for independence and the history of Ireland to be free of British rule. Slowly I began to feel the stirrings of patriotism and identify with the lofty ideals and values of the people who were the founders of the United States.

Slowly I found myself stirred by the words of *The Star Spangled Banner*. I enthusiastically joined in…

Oh say does that Star Spangled Banner yet wave

O'er the land of the free and the home of the brave.

The school system was fulfilling one of its missions, the assimilation of new immigrants.

Abraham Lincoln in the Gettysburg Address spoke these famous words; "Of the people, by the people and for the people." For the Fourth of July we were required to write an essay about a famous American and I expressed all my idealistic enthusiasm for "Honest Abe" in four handwritten pages. The phrase, "All men are created equal" was real and slavery was a mockery of that belief. I wrote passionately of this great president who freed the slaves and became a symbol of what it meant to be an American citizen. The Citizenship Medal was awarded to me when I graduated from grammar school. I still keep it in my jewelry box and concluded it must have been that essay. Clearly it was also because of my growing acceptance of my new identity, Irish-American.

Dad introduced us to some of the finer things in New York. We took the subway to New York City and went to the top of the Empire State Building and then to the best lunch of all, Horn and Hardart's ('the Automat'). I had my own six quarters and carefully studied each box window full of different foods until I chose exactly what I wanted. I put the quarter in the slot and opened up the door for instant gratification. We went to Coney Island and I rode on the roller coaster with him beside me. I hung onto his tie the entire ride and nearly choked him. Mom took us shopping to Gimbel's and Macy's and for special bargains, to Klein's on Union Square.

Besides assimilation into American culture, Catholic school had the same secondary mission as Ireland, to recruit nuns and priests.

When I filled out questionnaires in grammar school, I always answered the question, "What do you want to be in the future?" with "Become a nun." They didn't have to work too hard on me.

We were unabashedly told, "Marriage is 100% and entering religious life is 110%." I felt satisfied by the higher percentage choice I made. Neither parent pushed the convent. On the contrary, it was looked upon as a phase that would pass. But I quietly internalized everything I was told by the nuns.

I fell in love with the unconventional nuns in particular. Sister Robert Michael made you love history, and between lessons, while still in the classroom, she taught the girls how to throw softball.

"Place your fingers on the laces and your thumb underneath. Everything you do has to be in line with your target. Remember, the tighter the spin, the better the rotation of the ball. Elbow high and let it fly."

We took turns using our own newly-acquired leather mitts, and threw softballs from the front of the room to the back. I loved the sound of the smack of the ball in my mitt. The trick was not to hit the statue of the Blessed Virgin Mary about four feet tall hanging on the wall to the right, or your classmates sitting in neat rows to the left. The BVM dressed in her light blue gown was hit a few times but never fell off. I thought because of that, she was all in favor of ball playing beneath her virginal feet. When someone came to the door, Sister Robert Michael would put both hands behind her back with her mitt still on and say with a smile, "Can I help you?" We loved seeing her secret rebelliousness shared only with us.

We formed a team and I was the pitcher. She gave us the chance to feel the exhilaration of playing ball and experience new confidence in ourselves.

Walking down Woodside Avenue one day with my mother, she suddenly looked my way and said, "What's wrong? Why are you limping?"

I answered, "Oh, I don't know. It just started happening," and continued to limp down the street.

This went on for about a week. Sister Robert Michael had a limp as well.

The '60s were a time of great change, and idealism was at a peak. About 10% of our eighth-grade class was either planning to join religious life as a priest, brother or nun and another 10% were going into organizations like the Peace Corps. We were a sub-group within the class and spoke openly of our intentions. I trudged off to 7 a.m. mass at St. Sebastian's and watched the nuns walk up the aisle in twos and take their seats in the front rows. I loved watching them move in unison, joined together in prayer and song, sharing what was the holiest of callings in life.

Most of us were on the honor roll but we did not get high grades in behavior. I was a pious tomboy. I was religious and rebellious. My friends and I frequently got "needs improvement" for behavior on our report cards. Oddly, this was not inconsistent with the desire to become a nun or the desire on the nuns' parts to have us enter their community.

In the eighth grade three of us decided that it was time to check out the convent or the cloistered area where the nuns lived, as it was forbidden for anyone else to enter.

"Since we were moving in, why not get a preview?" I said.

We planned the break-in with the calculation of professional thieves. We covertly staked out the place to observe the best time and day to enter the premises.

It was Saturday at 9 a.m. A station wagon exited the rear parking lot filled with Sisters of Charity: All known nuns accounted for. Cloister break-in planned through hidden door in back of classroom coat closet. School premises easily breached. Convent entered one by one by perpetrators wearing sneakers.

"What if one of the nuns is still inside?" whispered Cassie.

"They're all out for a few hours," I said, my heart pounding with fear. "Hurry, but be quiet. Let's see as much as we can."

Doors were opened along the hallways to the library and private bedrooms, all looking fairly comfortable and livable. The bedrooms even had mirrors. Nice long dining room table polished to a high gloss. Our own blurred images reflected back at us.

"What's that in the corner?" asked Rosemary. We froze.

I took a step forward. "It's a statue, a life size statue of the Sacred Heart. Oh God. It looks real in the dark."

"Yeah. Especially with his hands reaching out to us," Rosemary said.

"Let's go," I said.

We now saw what was on the other side of the cloistered walls. All exited undetected.

The following Monday evening when I was helping our eighth grade teacher, Sister Agnes Carmella with the Sunday Mass donation envelopes, she turned to me and said, "We know you broke into the convent." I was stunned.

She followed up with, "It's like someone breaking into your home. There was a nun who stayed in the convent in bed that day because she was not feeling well. We saw your sneaker prints all over the floors. Don't you feel guilty?"

I answered her with a direct look. "No. I feel relieved." She knew what I meant and why I so brazenly said it. To my amazement, the subject was dropped.

The only thing that stood between me and the convent was high school. It seemed like an unnecessary intrusion into my clearly laid out plans. There was no choice. I could not be a high school drop out because I wanted to enter the convent. So I took Latin for four years. I was a member of the National Catholic Forensic League and placed as a finalist two different years. Sister Mary Anthony was my speech instructor and challenged me to have a presence and deliver a dramatic and compelling presentation. We won trips to Miami and Atlantic City for national competitions. When I placed among the top twenty-five nationally, Sister Anthony had tears rolling down her face. I believe now it was because her own dream was disintegrating as she watched mine begin, and within a few short years she left religious life.

The Sisters of Mercy were strong teachers and moralists on Catholic tradition and very connected to each of their students personally. Sister Bridget was my homeroom teacher one year and she spoke to me about my "vocation to religious life." It was she who said, "I have an instinct for those students who are called to religious life. When I saw you walk to the front of the stage in your red velvet dress and speak a solo part at the Christmas pageant, I knew you would be a nun."

Ironically in my senior year, she was the same person who told me angrily, because I refused to pick up her keys, that I was an "iconoclast" and "not suitable for the convent." I looked up iconoclast and learned it meant, "a breaker of images." I liked it.

Surely this is all part of having a higher calling.

Last-ditch efforts were made to have me wait or question my decision, but I could not be deterred.

Dad asked, "Do you want to go to medical school? We'll work it out."

I said, "I do not. The convent will send me to school."

Grainne was living in England studying nursing and I only had a few brief exchanges with her on the phone.

It basically went like, "I can't believe you're really doing this," over and over.

She had been living the bohemian life before she took off for England, dressed in black from head to toe, smoking cigarettes and studying at the Art Students League in N.Y.C. I became more religious by the week and insisted on wearing only navy blue or brown in preparation for my life of austerity. We couldn't have been more opposite. I began reading the lives of the saints and heavier theology like *The Confessions of Saint Augustine.*

Thou hast made us for Thyself, O Lord, and our hearts are restless until they rest in Thee.

It was in my junior year that my resolve to become a nun took a different turn. A group of us began volunteering at a Catholic home for the aged in New York City. The Carmelite Nuns who ran it were different...more accessible. More relaxed.

More fun. We were called Carmelettes. The weekends didn't come fast enough. Every weekend, from 9 a.m. until 4 p.m. we worked on the units in the nursing home under the supervision of one of the sisters who ran the unit. We shaved the men, helped the residents to activities, cleaned, served meals and did whatever else was needed. We loved it.

One day Mom said, "I wish you could spend some of that time doing things around here to help me."

It was not long before we became assigned to specific nuns and the nursing units they ran. I fell in love with Sister Monica. She was young, playful, smart, sexy and loved the residents. At some point each weekend we would steal away privately to talk about religious life and life in general. She was my mentor and confidant and influenced my developing views on just about everything. I made the decision that this was the order I would be entering after high school. Sister Monica challenged my decision by suggesting, "Why not wait a year and explore more of the world? "

I can't bear the thought of waiting another year.

"It's not an easy life. You can't know what that means until you are behind the convent walls."

I want to dedicate my life to God. I know it isn't going to be easy. Being part of the community of sisters, sharing the same love and the same calling is all I need. All I want.

"I want to be a Bride of Christ, like you. Throughout my life, I have been waiting for this. I am called to a life of service and sacrifice in religious life. I know this is what I want."

She replied, "I know. I felt the same way before I entered. I would love to be your sponsor to enter our order. It seems clear that you are called, like I was. You know I love you, don't you?"

"I do," I replied, beaming with joy.

I secretly questioned how I got this compelling call to enter the convent. Was it an auditory hallucination, a voice within guiding me, my subconscious planning my next life experience? I don't know. But I did know I had gotten the call.

As an afterthought, Sister Monica lovingly advised, "Just think about it some more before you apply. While you're doing that my brother is in the Navy and needs a pen pal. Here's his address. Why don't you write to him?"

I took his address and wrote to him, thrilled that she was sharing her younger brother with me. We corresponded for a year and met up when he was on leave. He came to our house in Woodside. Gene was very handsome, all spiffed up in his sailor uniform. It was terribly uncomfortable. I felt like I was in a 19th century courting parlor under the watchful eye of my family. We had tea and biscuits brought into our formal living room by Mom. My Aunt Mary rushed over to get a peek at him. She was titillated, even during her years of senility, by matters of the heart. I believe the idea of an American sailor really launched her boat. She made statements to any young person like, "Do you have a boyfriend? When are you getting married? I should never have married my husband. Johnny Cullane was the one I should have married."

With Gene and I, there were no sparks flying. Perhaps we would have had an actual date had I not told him directly that I was entering the convent in six months. Poor guy. I did the mandatory Senior Prom and dated superficially for a while in my senior year but I clearly and consistently had other pressing priorities. Another love waiting. Another calling.

Chapter 8

April 15, 1967

Dear Mother Justine, O. Carm:

I am writing this letter to request admission to the Order of the Carmelites. I have been a Carmelette and have come to love the life and work of the Carmelite Order. Since the age of eight, I have felt called to religious life to serve God. My senior year in high school will end in June of this year and I would like to join your community as a postulant the following September.

You will find in me someone who will work hard to be committed to religious life and embrace the vows of poverty, chastity and obedience.

Please consider my request and let me know the next steps I need to take so that I may answer God's call.

Sincerely,

Maeve Walsh

A response letter arrived within two weeks from the Motherhouse. With it was an application and request for letters of recommendation. Everything was completed and returned within a week. In May I received a larger envelope detailing a letter of acceptance, the date and time of my entrance and a list of what should be included in my trousseau. At last, I was going to become a nun. I embarked on the second transformation, one that would call for a major metamorphosis of my identity.

It never occurred to me to research the history of the Carmelite order or any of the other monastic communities I met along the way. Many of the practices and rules in the mid-twentieth century dated back to the fifteenth. Each religious order had its own set of rules and customs, overseen in modern times by the Vatican.

There is a spiritual link between the ancient prophet Elijah and the Carmelite order. Elijah's memory was kept alive on Mount Carmel where he challenged the people to follow Yahweh, the true God in the epic story of Elijah confronting the prophets of Baal. Elijah embarked on a long journey through the desert. He began to despair and called out to God that he wanted to die. God told him to continue his journey to Mount Horeb where God made himself known to Elijah. God did not reveal himself in the usual ways found in the Old Testament such as

115

fire, earthquake and storm, but in the sound of a gentle breeze: almost silence. The Carmelite way of life speaks of listening to the will of God in the unexpected and in silence. It speaks to being led by the Spirit that has taken root in each heart.

Mother Justine was the founder of the Order of Carmelites. Born to Catholic parents in Ireland, she became a Little Sister of the Poor who cared for the destitute elderly in Europe. The order sent her to the Bronx to be a superior of a home for the aged. Driven by dissatisfaction with the care of the elderly she experienced in the United States, she was dispensed from her vows for the purpose of starting a new order of nuns. With a handful of other sisters on the eve of the Great Depression of 1929, in affiliation with an order of Carmelite Brothers, she opened her own sisterhood. They were called the Carmelite Sisters. They were an active order meaning they were engaged in a service as opposed to a contemplative order that is cloistered and not engaged in a profession like teaching or nursing. During her lifetime she opened forty-nine homes, including one in Ireland and one in Scotland. To all who knew her, she was a humble and kind woman, truly and simply dedicated to the care of the aged. Her gift was seeing Christ in each aged person.

Since her early ventures in forming her own order, she forged close relationships with bishops and priests in her diocese and saw them as embodiments of Christ on earth. She was a religious traditionalist. During the time of Vatican II when religious orders were challenged to abandon antiquated traditions, she stood firm for holding onto traditional customs and training of new religious.

She is quoted as saying, "Stay with Rome is my advice to you during these days of confusion and change. We must live the Carmelite life. Prayer, humility, charity, mortification, silence, unselfishness and community life will always be necessary to preserve the spirit of religious life."

She encouraged her professed nuns working in the field, "Do all possible to encourage young girls to enter our community. It is up to you . . . by your religious example to attract girls to it." And so they did.

I counted the days and hours much like a young bride to be would count the days to her wedding. I began to assemble the items listed in *What to Bring With You …* things that were worn by a nineteenth century peasant girl: nightdresses with long sleeves, old fashioned white only undergarments found in the very back of a lingerie store (and I am not referring to Victoria's Secret), long black stockings, sturdy black oxfords, men's undershirts, a dark brown cardigan, a brown or black shawl, and unscented toiletries. The trousseau was completely practical and basic and I never gave it a second thought. My friends threw me a shower. Really. I talked about wanting to be called Sister Augustine and one of the gifts was a white cotton T-shirt with the words, "Sr. Augie" on the front. The convent provided the Postulant outfit and the Novice habit. The habits were re-cycled as new bodies stepped forward to be consecrated to God. Other bodies inhabited them in the past, other souls with the same calling as myself. They prayed and contemplated and served within the folds that soon would envelop me. Perhaps they left religious life to return to the world. Perhaps they died in the service of the Lord. The call of God filled my heart and my mind on a daily basis. Sister Monica embraced my resolve to enter right after high school.

So the question might be asked, "What do you do with your time just before you enter a convent where you plan to stay for the remainder of your life?" Dad and I went on a one week trip to Mexico that summer. He worked for the airlines and it's from him I got my love of travel. We went to Mexico City and a few surrounding towns. Perhaps he thought seeing more of the world might change my mind about entering an enclosure with ancient practices grounded in self-denial. He was an agnostic after all and he was about to give up his youngest daughter to the service of God. On my request we actually visited an ancient Carmelite Church outside of Mexico City. It was a hot day and I wore shorts . . . long shorts. Inside the church, as we approached the Station of the Cross, Jesus Meets the Women of Jerusalem, we were accosted by an elderly, black clothed Mexican woman, yelling in Spanish and waving at us.

Dad said, "It's because you are not dressed properly. She should only know where you're going in a few weeks."

We didn't mean to be disrespectful to her customs, but we did laugh together about it. He surely was a good sport taking me there.

September 8th, 1967 arrived. I entered the convent for the rest of my life. I was awake at the crack of dawn. Dad wrote the following poem. He did so because, despite being an agnostic, he offered his love and support for my dream.

I am glad I stayed around awhile

To see you in God's State

And watch your eyes reflect His smile

As he meets you at the gate.

I know that he will hold your hand

And guide you all the way

To keep you in His Holy Band

And watch you gently pray.

So when your thoughts drift through the years

As you meditate and pray

Let love and joy replace those tears

And smile with Him each day.

Mom & Dad

My family drove me to Saint Andrew's Home in the Bronx where I would spend my postulancy with twenty-five other new recruits. The postulancy is a time of probation, a time for testing a new candidate for suitability. The postulant experienced a religious life of prayer and study and the work of the community.

The first day was a blur. Individually we were escorted to the convent area, dressed in our postulant outfits of brown dress and short black veil. Our clothes from the world were boxed away as we took the first step in assuming our new identities. The clothes themselves shaped our new identity. Sameness accepted. Uniqueness abandoned. One collective persona formed. Individuality sacrificed in service to God, in service to the community.

I did not comprehend the complexity, the far-reaching daily effects of the willing yet unknown sacrifice at hand. We were all young white women, from different parts of the United States and Canada, under the age of 24, excited and thrilled to be joining the Carmelite Order. We felt chosen. We walked in procession down the aisle of the small chapel, as our families waited to witness our transformation. Sacred organ music and voices washed away our previous lives and permeated our willing souls.

Veni Sancte Spiritus (Come Holy Spirit) sung by the choir of professed nuns in Latin.

Cleanse that which is unclean,	*Lava quod est sordidum,*
Water that which is dry,	*Riga quod est aridum*
Heal that which is wounded.	*Sana quod est saucium.*
Bend that which is inflexible,	*Flecte quod est rigidum,*
Fire that which is chilled,	*Fove quod est frigidum*
Correct what goes astray .	*Rege quod est devium.*
Grant the reward of virtue,	*Da tuis fidelibus*

Grant the deliverance of salvation. In te confidentibus,

Grant eternal joy.   Sacrum septenarium.

The postulants speak the words in unison, "I desire to begin the time of discernment - the time of listening to God as He speaks in and through the Community. I ask for your prayers that I may spend the rest of my life in His Eucharistic Presence and prepare my soul for the great day of union between bride and Bridegroom."

We said goodbye to family. Dinner and introductions were made in the community room and our Postulant Mistress provided an initial orientation. Vespers (at the lighting of the lamps) is part of the Divine Office or evening set of prayers and hymns. A beautiful voice of a newly professed nun intoned a Latin chant, followed by the assembly of nuns repeating the words in the same tone. Repeated stanzas were sung standing, sitting, and standing again. The notes filled the small chapel. Even the tone deaf were swept away by this sea of mesmerizing sound.

The dormitory contained our assigned cubicles with a bed and side table, surrounded by white curtains, pulled at night around a space large enough to stand, dress and undress. Never to be alone. Always to be supervised. Grand Silence began at nine and lasted until after breakfast the following morning. You did not speak and learned to practice custody of the eyes.

Dormitory sleeping was a real equalizer. I listened to the sounds of soft cries, bodily emissions, turning bodies on the not-so-comfortable and unfamiliar beds and people talking in their sleep. But I was very happy to be present on my own bed within the company of my new sisters. Some were smart and true Baby Boomers, bursting with the excitement of the opportunity to change the world. Some were dull and low achievers, finding a place in a world that would both accept and elevate them. A small few were mentally ill or at least, vulnerable souls. We all were one. Sisters in Jesus Christ.

We rose at 5:30 a.m., dressed in silence and began the day with Matins (of or belonging to the morning). This is the first set of prayers followed by celebration of the Eucharist and breakfast. The entire community remained in silence except for the prayers and hymns in the Chapel. The day was filled with work assignments and the silence rule was not required. Exuberant young women could let loose, lost in their chores and lessons of service.

The first week was the honeymoon, allowing us to get the hang of the schedule and learn what would be expected. The postulant mistress, Sister Boniface, was smart, fun loving and approachable. A couple of months into our postulancy, one of the postulants approached me and asked if we could speak privately.

"Of course," I said. We met on the landing overlooking a front garden.

"I can't speak to just anyone about this, but I have to tell you. The Blessed Virgin has appeared to me twice and has spoken to me. She wants me to build a chapel right over there," she said, pointing to a crowded spot on the lawn in front of the window.

Ok. I have a real problem here. What do I do? I don't believe in apparitions or religious sightings. Why me? Is she hallucinating?

"She spoke to you through the window?" I asked.

"Yes. She promised peace would come to the world through the Carmelite Order."

"I see. I don't know what to say. Are you sure you saw an actual figure?"

"Yes. Standing in the sky over there in a blue gown, holding a globe."

"It's . . . ahm . . . amazing. Let's talk to Sister Boniface," I stammered.

"No. I'll see the Blessed Virgin again, I'm sure. I can't tell her now."

She believed she was called as a special envoy to have a chapel built on the grounds, where clearly one already existed. I felt scared to sleep in a dormitory with her and asked to speak with Sister Boniface as soon as possible.

"She is scary and needs help. I am afraid this is just the beginning," I reported. Sister Boniface listened, thanked me and within a day this particular postulant was gone. This was the time to weed out unsuitable candidates for religious life, but I felt badly that I was the messenger or at the very least, tilted the scale. I hope that she received the help she needed when she returned home.

Religious life was intense. The isolation experienced through daily contemplation and silence was too much for anyone 'on the edge' to endure. Solitude was a catalyst for unhinged behavior. What is the boundary between delusions and faulty thinking? Where is it safe to suspend realistic and logical thinking? Is the mind protected just because a religious organization deems fantastic stories believable when it comes to matters of faith? I wondered if there was a psychological screening process for entrance to religious life. Someone's mental health might be placed at risk. I didn't have a mental health screening. Perhaps it could not be accurately assessed prior to the real intensity of the experience? On second thought, even years later, the psychiatric profession did not possess the tools nor skills to identify any more than the blatantly dysfunctional.

One of my pleasures was being assigned to read during meals while the professed nuns and postulants ate in silence. A few of us read on a regular basis. Mother Superior announced a non-silent meal on Sundays, holidays and other times; otherwise, we read from the Bible or theology, all quite boring and conservative. My surviving Irish lilt added a touch of interest and I filled the words with as much emotional meaning as possible. After Grace was said before meals, we sat and the Superior knocked on the table. At that point the reader stood, walked to the center of the refectory, faced the head table and bowed to the Superior before walking to the reading lectern. I had a problem with this and so I did not bow the first number of times. Instead I delivered a fast nod and moved to the lectern. Once I pretended to trip on a chair leg to camouflage my blatant refusal to stop and bow to another human being. My strategy made my avoidance all the more visible. Giggles erupted from the postulant's table. The lips of Mother Superior curled involuntarily, suppressing her own need to laugh and ended in a look of disapproval.

Sister Boniface informed me, "You have no choice about bowing. You bow to the Superior out of respect. She is the representative of Christ for our religious house."

This was all part of establishing conformity, humility and obedience. I did it but I didn't like it.

And then I had an epochal moment. It was one that would force me to look at my intentions and motivations smack dead center. On a Saturday afternoon about six weeks before the end of the Postulancy and the beginning of the Novitiate, Sister Boniface called me into her office, a small cubbyhole underneath the stairs.

She said, "I need to tell you something that will be upsetting to you. Sister Monica left our community last week. I know she is your sponsor and you were close."

I sat in shock.

What?? Why? She's gone? Left the Carmelites, my new family? Our family?

I was totally thrown, abandoned, betrayed.

Sister Boniface said, "You will need some time to think about this and take it in. It is a great loss but she felt she needed to leave."

"Can I talk to her?" I asked.

"No. This is something you have to get through on your own. Take the rest of today and tomorrow off, except for morning mass."

I went straight to my cell/curtain space and got into bed. I cried and cried. I couldn't stop, even though I knew the sounds carried through the dormitory. I slept. I cried again. I prayed to Christ about my feelings, asking for insight and direction. I had a long talk with myself about my vocation.

Your vocation is independent of Sister Monica. You have to be here for God and for yourself only. That is your choice. If this shakes your vocation, then you never had one.

Psychologically it was all the more painful by the rules of no communication with the outside world and particularly a person who left the community. Silence. Separation. I struggled with the meaning of this profound loss of a person I loved and who loved me. I went to the Chapel and prayed before the tabernacle and the large crucifix of Christ on the cross in the background. A light burned above the tabernacle to remind us of God's living presence.

Please give me the inner light to clear my mind and purify my thoughts.

Slowly, as I meditated, I felt God's warmth and love within me. It was an intense feeling, physically as well as spiritually. My heart opened up and absorbed that love, and a unity with Christ enveloped me.

The words of St John of the Cross, a sixteenth century mystic came to mind.

Oh living flame of love.

How tenderly you force

To my soul's innermost core your fiery probe.

Oh lamps of fiery blaze

To whose refulgent fuel

The deepest caverns of my soul grow bright.

The deepest caverns of my soul grow bright . . .

I made the choice to stay. God spoke to me in the silence. Celestial conversation. His love had taken root in my soul.

Sister Boniface and I discussed my thinking and even though I thought of Sister Monica many times, I separated my connection in terms of my own religious life and calling. A transformation made possible by the presence of Divine love.

Chapter 9

In April the postulancy ended with twenty-two of us ready to take the chartered bus ride to the Novitiate. The eighty-six acre property is located on the east bank of the Hudson River with the Catskill Mountains rising beautifully in the not-too distant west. After three days of retreat, we boarded the bus for the Taconic Parkway to Upstate New York. There we would be wedded to Christ and begin a truly cloistered life during our next period of transformation. We passed over the Rip Van Winkle Bridge and I had visions of Ichabod Crane and the Headless Horseman of Sleepy Hollow as we approached our new home.

I stayed with thoughts of Rip Van Winkle and how he fell asleep for twenty years underneath a young, shady tree in these very hills.

God knows, exclaimed Rip, at his wits end after he awoke;
I'm not myself - I'm somebody else - that's me yonder - no -
that's somebody else got into my shoes - I was myself last night,
but I fell asleep on the mountain . . . and everything's changed,
and I'm changed, and I can't tell what's my name, or who I am.

When he awoke, the young tree he had fallen asleep under had matured. The world had changed. He didn't know who he was.

Sitting beside me, Sister Theresa grabbed my arm and yelled, "There's the sign for the Motherhouse."

Her face beamed. I awoke from my reverie about Rip van Winkle to the gated entrance of my new home and threw the window open.

We eased up the long driveway to the Motherhouse estate. It was lined with birch, ash and hemlock trees. The bus driver took his time, allowing us to get our last glimpse of the world before he delivered us to the Lord. A sweet woody smell engulfed us. The trees formed a sacred corridor along the path ahead. The hemlocks towered and cast a dense shade as they led us forward. They stood as symbols of transformation and living proof of survival and longevity. Clusters of birch trees, young and old, offered their own messages scrawled on the silver bark, peeled and scattered on the ground.

We know of new beginnings. We know of separation and new life.

The ash trees swayed silently in the breeze. They showed the beginning of new buds, new life, and an early spring.

We would not even walk to the end of this driveway in the years ahead. It just wouldn't occur to us. The stately white mansion appeared at the end of the drive and a group of white veiled novices in a cluster waited to welcome the newcomers. Two black-veiled professed sisters stood in front when the doors of the bus opened. We poured out to smiles and hugs and "Welcome to your new home."

Every change of season and weather, indeed, every hour of the day, produced a change in the magical hues and shapes of the Catskill Mountains. Blue and purple reflected from them on that day. A blanket of gray vapors gathered about their tops, and in the last rays of the setting sun, they were lit up like a crown of glory. It was divine. There was a sense of expectation and freshness in the air and a landscape conducive to holiness, meditation and serenity.

We were welcomed and shown to our individual rooms, a big step up from dormitory living. Mine was at the end of the hall and consisted of a bed, a desk, a nightstand and a closet. I often sat on the deep window sill that looked out on the Hudson River rushing past us. A small crucifix hung over the bed. A cell of my own. A silent cell. I was elated.

Anticipation was high as we participated in preparations for becoming novices in our Reception Ceremony the following weekend. The Novitiate Wedding Dress Collection was truly heavenly. The dresses had none of the opulence of a Coco Chanel collection but more of a Grace Kelly traditional, satin elegance with long sleeves, floor length skirt and high neck. We were each matched to wedding dresses that fit with the assistance of the senior novices, all of us giddy with excitement. Nervous brides-to-be. The dresses hung patiently packed away from year to year in the Motherhouse Bridal closet, always making a fresh appearance on Reception Day for a few moments of fame. We practiced walking as we wobbled about in our white high-heeled shoes. I was sure I would fall over as I approached the marriage altar.

Mother Justine met with us privately to discuss our new name in religious life, which would be given to us at our Reception Ceremony. She was a bit like the Wizard of Oz

134

behind the curtain, inaccessible, glorified. In person she was a solid presence, gentle and strong at the same time. She had a soft face with apple round cheeks, a penetrating gaze enlarged by her rimless glasses.

"Are you sure you want to become a nun?" she asked.

"I am, Mother."

"What name would you like in religious life?"

Well rehearsed, I replied, "Sister Augustine, Mother."

She hesitated. "I was thinking you might keep your own name, Maeve."

I was shocked. Unprepared. Part of the whole allure was taking on a new identity, leaving the world behind. A new name was the public symbol of this metamorphosis along with wearing the habit. It was a stage name, so to speak, for the performance of being a nun.

Oh no, no, no.

I replied, "I really want Sister Augustine as I love this saint and what he had to say.

Love God and do what you will . . . He who sings prays twice.

I voiced my own will with the Mother General of the Community, the Foundress.

She said quietly, "Very well, it will be Sister Augustine."

I said only, "Thank you, Mother."

In the past, there probably would not have been a choice of a new name. It would have been assigned. She wanted me to keep my Irish given name that I grew to love in later years. Maybe she liked the name or perhaps she sensed I would always just be Maeve. She was giving me a gift. I just couldn't hear it at the time. Saint Augustine, I learned later in life was a misogynist, a person who hated or strongly disliked women.

We practiced our responses for the ceremony of receiving the habit and voicing our intention to become Brides of Christ. A rehearsal dinner attended by the brides and their convent superiors. No maids of honor. No partying into the late hours of the night. A priest, the representative of Christ on earth, would perform the actual ceremony.

If cleanliness is next to godliness, then the Motherhouse chapel had to be very close to heaven. It was always pristine, but on Reception Day for the new novices, it sparkled. The pure white altar linens were starched to just the right amount of firmness and lay delicately in place. Lilies of the Valley with blue Forget-Me-Nots adorned the statue of Our Lady of Mount Carmel on the side altar. Small golden yellow flowers and Baby's Breath were unobtrusively arranged in vases in front of the altar. "Simplicity is the soul of elegance" was the motto of divine decorative style.

The entire nave was bathed in warm hues as the sun shone through the stained glass windows from the east. I watched the patterns they created wander across the floor and touch the veils of sisters kneeling in prayer in front of me. I wondered how the glass was made and how such delicate beauty survived the onslaught of winter winds year after year.

The chapel was packed with friends and family. Mine were jammed together in a pew as close to the altar and to each other as they could get to witness the ceremony. Many had come from far away and actually woke up this morning at the Rip Van Winkle Motor Lodge and continued on to the Motherhouse. Visiting nuns and senior novices were in their assigned seats and the choir mistress was softly playing *Be Thou But Near* by Johann Sebastian Bach on the organ.

We lined up outside the back of the chapel, paired in twos in our wedding attire, waiting nervously for the signal to begin our walk down the aisle to join our invisible groom. Suddenly the music changed and the voices of the nuns echoed those of

Mary in the singing of the first words of the *Magnificat*, an ancient Christian Jewish hymn of praise for God. The first twosome in line began the long walk down the aisle and all heads turned to witness the procession to the altar. The looks were those of amazement and disbelief, tears of joy from proud parents giving their daughters to God and tears of loss, knowing they could never share in the lives that were chosen by their children. My gaze fell downward as I began my walk and I timed my steps in sequence with the wobbly white shoes directly in front of me. The *Magnificat* was, to me, a love song.

My soul glorifies the Lord, and my spirit rejoices in God, my Savior.

The priest stood richly adorned in gold vestments, waiting to solemnize our commitment to the Church, our marriage to Christ. My eyes met my mother's in loving acknowledgement and I gave Dad a nodding quick smile. Both of them were in tears.

The service began with words and responses in Latin, making what was about to happen seem all the more ancient and mysterious.

As we knelt at the altar railing the priest asked, "What do you seek?"

We answered in unison, "The grace of God and the habit of holy religion."

He continued, "Do you truly desire to enter the state of holy religion?"

We replied, "I desire it with all my heart."

"Do you intend to follow the rules of the Carmelite Order?"

Response, "I do intend with the help of Divine Grace."

We rose and formed a line to slowly walk back down the aisle and exit the church to an adjoining room where an ancient ritual was reenacted - the dressing of a Carmelite novice. It couldn't happen fast enough. I raised my arms as Conspirators in Christ slipped the satin wedding gown off my consenting body.

I was transformed, garment-by-garment, deeper and deeper into the cloistered life. I was shown how to put my face through the starched white hood, pull it tightly to the back of my head and secure it in place with straight pins. A starched white band covered my forehead and was tied in the back of my head, my short hair now permanently covered. Next I lifted on the large brown habit and secured it at the waist with a belt. The guimpe or stiff breast piece extended to a neck collar that was pinned at the back of my neck. The scapular of Our Lady of Mount Carmel was placed over my shoulders and pinned in place. A white veil was placed on my head and the folds neatly arranged by pinning sections to my headpiece. My hearing immediately diminished and my side view of the world was obliterated. That was the goal. The off-white celebratory cloak of Carmel was placed over my shoulders and hung to the floor.

We reentered the chapel wearing the habit and white veil of a novice, ready to leave the world behind. My body felt weighted down. The silence was audible. The ceremony continued to celebrate new life in Jesus Christ and death to the world. Part of the traditional ritual is the taking of a new name, leaving your family name behind. Two by two we entered the sanctuary and lay prostrate on the floor to signify our acceptance of death to the world, arms outstretched in imitation of Christ's death on the cross. Our new names were spoken.

"You will now be known as Sister Mary Augustine."

How will I get up from here? I'm buried, tangled in folds of heavy brown serge flattened against the floor in a church filled to the rafters.

Suddenly I felt the enormity of my choice. Murmurs of responsive prayer by the congregation reached my ears, but the words were muffled.

My bride partner is half way up. I better move.

Somehow I managed to rise and return, eyes cast downward, to my seat.

The choir began the *Regnum Mundi*, traditionally sung in ceremonies of embracing religious life to signify acceptance of dying to the world.

"I despise the kingdom of the world, and all the beauty of the world, for love of the Lord Jesus Christ: whom I see, whom I love, in whom I believe, in whom I delight."

The shadow of a small bird was perched on a branch outside the clear cathedral stained glass window of Our Lady of Mount Carmel. From my aisle seat, I could see it bobbing up and down in the light blue folds of her gown. It sang its own song in spurts of high and soft sounds. I was distracted by it but loved its accompaniment with the sacred music. It seemed to be singing, "Not all the beauty of the world do you have to despise. Look at me. Listen to me. Remember me."

The priest began the Benediction as the ceremony came to a close. The chapel was filled with the smell of incense penetrating the well-worn wooden pews and old woolen habits. It had a numbing and dizzying effect. We were now new brides of Christ about to begin the reality of the training period of the Novitiate. The final song, *Ecce Quam Bonum* from Psalm 133, accompanied us as we walked out, as novices, to the love of family, new and old. Our professed sisters welcomed us into their dwelling, greeting us with the liturgical PAX or kiss of peace.

We met in the large auditorium where tables were set and senior novices served a small lunch. While I was so happy to see my family and friends, in a strange way I already felt separated from them. I smiled my new nunly smile and accepted the compliments as to how beautiful I looked in the habit. I was aware that any personal beauty I possessed should be unimportant and yet it pleased me. My family would know me less and less as I in-habited my new persona. We had even been instructed on how to hold our hands inside the sleeves of our habit. Little did they know how afraid I was to move my head, lest I get impaled by a straight pin. I did love being in the habit. I felt holy. Two worlds collided within me; the I of eighteen years with the family I loved, and me in my new religious family of adult choosing.

Families were getting ready to leave, when I caught sight of a figure in a black veil standing above the floor in the center area of the stage. She seemed to be actively surveying the new recruits, unbeknownst to them. She had the build of a quarterback, the stern face of a general beginning a campaign: thin lips, tightly pressed, attentive as a red tailed hawk about to capture its prey. Reflexively, I chose to break through the moment and gave this formidable figure a head salute of friendly deference. Not a muscle moved in response but her brain registered me, as if to say,

This is one that will need special breaking in, special scrutiny.

Big mistake on my part. Unknowingly I had allowed myself to stand out, and this was the first violation of not blending in, of asserting my personality. A challenge filled the room. I did not know she was the Mistress of Novices. She was the one responsible for making me die to myself, to my former life.

"For whosoever will save his life shall lose it; but whosoever shall lose his life for my sake, shall save it."
Matthew 16: 21-28.

That was the goal of the Novitiate - to lose the self, the ego. To submit to the will of God as voiced through your superiors and the Holy Rule. To be molded as a piece of clay is molded in another's hands, yielding and submitting with unquestioning blind obedience. To be reformed. To be transformed. Only by doing so could Jesus become my all. Only by emptying myself to do His will could I grow closer to God. Although I knew I was choosing to sacrifice my life in the world to become a nun, I never anticipated the extent of having to renounce myself as an individual. De-individuation was the goal of convent living.

Our loved ones left us . . . or we left them. We would not see them or speak to them for at least a year. Letters received were read or screened before they reached us and our letters out were likewise screened. Newspapers and magazines were things of the past and TV news or shows did not exist. All connection with the outside world was gone. If a national crisis occurred, the Mother General and Novice Mistress would decide what we needed to know, if anything. The cloistered life was iron-clad, rigorous and inflexible. We were for the most part idealistic, eager to please and accepting of our isolation from all things worldly.

The bird outside the chapel window at my Reception Ceremony must have known the sounds and voices of this time in history. Woodstock was only a short fly of twenty-five miles away from the convent. It was here in the rain and mud that music and songs by Janis Joplin and The Grateful Dead filled the sky. Unified voices opposed the Vietnam War, chants and demonstrations demanded civil rights for Black people, Asian people and women students. Smoking pot and experimentation with drugs was the thing to do. Traditional values were challenged and the saying "Do your own thing" became popularized. The sexual revolution provided choices to men and women around contraception and gender roles, not possible before. The world of the convent that I chose and the world of the '60s were centuries, perhaps millennia apart.

Chapter 10

My daily schedule went something like this:

Loud hand bell rung in the halls by an appointed novice at 5:30 am.

Jumped out of bed and use communal bathroom wearing small head veil with bathrobe.

Dressed in layers of habit using straight pins without a mirror.

Arrived in chapel in assigned place by 6:15 am.

Recited Matins. Sang hymns. Mass and Holy Communion.

Listened to reading while eating breakfast in silence. (Unless bell was rung by superior).

Attended morning class on Holy Rule of Carmelites.

Reported to work assignment in the refectory.

Listened to reading while eating lunch in silence. (Unless bell was rung by superior).

Attended choir practice, Mariology lecture (study of Mary) or other instruction.

Afternoon walk on grounds for 30 min. or free time.

Reported to work assignment.

Attended chapel for special prayers or devotion.

Listened to reading while eating dinner in silence. (Unless bell was rung by superior).

Recited Vespers in chapel.

Group recreation in common room for one hour. (We were allowed to talk).

Bedtime. Lights out by 9:00 or 9:30 p.m.

The mornings offered the most difficulty. Waking up, washing up, wrapping up in full habit in 45 minutes challenged my ability to dress as a nun. In this convent triathlon, I came in last over the finish line in the chapel each morning. The professed nuns and novices were assembled, quietly meditating when I rushed in, veil flying. Eyes watched me slide into the pew as I prayed for invisibility. Touching another sister was totally discouraged, but I often felt the novice behind me, rearranging my veil and straightening its folds. I closed my eyes, grateful for her help. After getting settled, I loved the songs and prayers in Latin, the rituals and Mass, the closeness of community. Sister Mary Aloysius, our Mistress of Novices pointed out my lateness and un-nunly deportment in our meetings.

"You hurry into chapel with your head pushed out in front. Sister, try to walk gently and hold your head up."

I loved choir. My father often said, "You can't carry a note in a bucket," in a fun-loving way, but I loved to sing. During choir practice I disappeared into myself. My voice synchronized with others and I lost myself to the whole. Individuality lost in this way produced an energy beyond words. It was both a physical and emotional release. We learned the sacred music of the different parts of the Mass, hymns for special church celebrations and the saying of the Office. Reciting of the Office included a prescribed set of prayers set by the Catholic Church at specific times of the day. The practice originated from Jewish prayers said at fixed times of the day in the Temple in Jerusalem when sacrifices were offered to God.

We confessed weekly. It had the purpose of receiving absolution from a priest for sins committed. Obviously we are talking minor or venial sins and the sins of most nuns were even one step below that. A nun's confession has been described as "being stoned to death with popcorn." How much sinning could you actually achieve in the convent? For me it was a challenge, thinking of what to confess, so I lied and made up plausible nunly sins.

"Bless me father for I have sinned. It's been one week since my last confession. I threw out food rather than finish dinner. I neglected to pray. I felt jealous of another sister when she was praised."

Sinning during confessions did make a bit of a mockery of the sacrament, but I had to go in with something.

Sometime during the early months of the Novitiate I approached the Mistress of Novices to turn over what was to me an important document, a full scholarship for a Bachelor's Degree from New York State. It would save the Order the expense of sending me to school and I was proud that I had achicved it.

"I want to give you this," I said. "It's a full scholarship to attend school after the Novitiate."

She looked at me, at the piece of paper, took it, opened a small top drawer on the right side of her desk, put it in and snapped it closed.

"We are not interested in this here."

"I thought you would be pleased," I replied, filled with surprise and disappointment.

This was a lesson in putting only God first; aspects of the world, especially the intellect was secondary.

Does she mean I may not be educated and free schooling would be forgotten? Lost? My achievement is unimportant?

The words of your superior and the rules of the Order represented the will of God and you had to obediently and humbly accept. It was shaping, transforming through humility and obedience. The self was unimportant. Something I had to work on obviously.

In the boardrooms of religious orders during this same time, debates occurred about the recent Vatican II documents calling on Catholic Orders to reexamine their missions and rules, including silence, wearing of traditional habits and training of novices. It was a call for a renewal of the Church and an examination of archaic systems in place in religious communities. As new recruits, we had no direct knowledge of the ideas being reviewed. In time I learned that my community, under the leadership of Mother Justine weighed in on the side of traditionalism. Fresh air with reformed ideas failed to enter its cloistered corridors.

Grand Silence was in effect from the end of Recreation the night before and continued through breakfast. Coffee, eggs, a little spiritual reading without talking to anyone is not such a bad idea early in the morning . . . Adhering to Grand Silence, its intent, its protections, its antiquity was one of the golden rules. I had a problem with it. One night before bed I entered the communal bathroom and found a novice in tears.

To hell with Grand Silence.

"Are you okay? What's wrong? It's okay to talk," I said.

We talked, witnessed by the silent and compliant.

The Jesus I was taught about in school would have stopped to talk, to comfort someone.

I was turned in by the righteous, and guess who had a problem with my failure to observe Grand Silence? Sister Mary

Aloysius, our Novice Mistress. I did try and most of the time I complied, but I continued to believe that exceptions had to be made.

I enjoyed working in the refectory. The refectory was the massive room where only nuns dined, all 100 plus of us, including professed nuns. It had a feudal feeling to it that I loved. The long wood tables were arranged in a U shape with the Mother General and other high ranking professed at the head table. You sat according to rank and longevity in the convent.

The newest novices set the hundred meal places and cleaned after the meal. The reader during meals sat at the reading lectern centrally located on the right side of the large room with two steps up to allow visibility to all present. An opened book lay on the slanted table. I learned the humble deportment required and read often with sincerity and poise. I had the bowing bit down by then. Servers dished out our food. You ate what the server placed on your plate. Most amazing, the food was great for institutional convent cuisine. At the end of the meal a stainless steel bowl was provided to each novice, lukewarm water poured into it, no soap and you washed your own dishes and utensils and dried them.

I remember wine served with meals on many occasions. Four-ounce glass portions were poured per person. Half of the novices didn't want the wine, so the crowd I hung with gestured to the non-drinkers, "Pass it down." We didn't know about fine wines. This was probably a Catholic version of Manischewitz, but it was wine. One Feast Day of Our Lady, we had wine-induced euphoria and luckily free time. Sister Carol and I went for a walk when suddenly she lay down in the middle of the road. She was a petite rotund novice from New Jersey. I pulled her off the road with all my might, down an incline where I watched her sleep for an hour. She flipped her headpiece off and I prayed that she would wake up and we would not be caught. I woke her up because we had to be back in the Chapel for a procession in honor of Our Lady and we were both in the lead holding lit candles. We bumped off the wall a few times as we drunkenly rounded the side aisles and sang our hearts out. We were overcome with devotion with a little help from the wine. It was another miracle that we did not get caught. She and I became good friends and looked forward to private conversations where we shared philosophies about religious life. We reinforced and strengthened our commitment in those talks and it helped us to understand and accept some of the more outdated aspects of the Novitiate training.

Unfortunately, it became clear that we were friends and the whole issue of 'particular friendships' came to the forefront. First, I don't know of any friendship that is not 'particular' and special. Religious organizations developed a hyper vigilant response to the possibility that friendship might advance to physical closeness and sex. Religious life attracts both gay and straight individuals in the priesthood, monasteries and convents. There is a strong need for denial of the former. It's also true that when individuals live together in intense and close communal settings, the need for physical closeness is common. I was inexperienced and unaware of my sexuality. My attractions were emotional and spiritual. While there was a small undercurrent of 'particular friendships' in the Novitiate, most women sublimated and repressed those feelings.

My counseling with the Novice Mistress focused on my interest in spending time with some sisters over others.

"When you walk into recreation in the evening, Sister Augustine, don't look in any particular direction, and sit down wherever you find yourself. You must look on all your sisters equally and spend time with them equally."

How do you do that? Equal in the sight of God . . . but they aren't all equal in terms of enjoying the one quickly passing hour of recreation. Some are painful to sit with and not much fun.

"The more you give your heart away to others, the less you have to give to God."

"The only way to God is through other people," I said in response.

"The emptier your heart is of other loves, the more God's love is available," she replied.

To me, this amounted to blasphemy. My beliefs had always been as clear and solid as the ground I walked on. I pictured the small snow globe Dad gave me exploding into a million pieces. I felt the pieces hitting that ground. Some of them wanted to shout out loud, didn't want to be ignored.

"Sister, this is not a choice. This is what is asked of you as a religious. It is something you need to work on. Spend time in the chapel praying and concentrating on the Holy Spirit to guide you."

"I will try, Mother," I responded.

I did try. It was useless. Awkward. Empty. I slipped back to looking where the fun people were, the people I had things in common with. I wasn't willing to continue to do something that felt absurd and impossible, day in and day out.

"Let's just agree to disagree," didn't ride well in the Novitiate. You needed to buy into the whole package. To my surprise and profound disappointment, I found power driven superiors and cliques of novices. Distorted, backward religious thinking created a lack of love and compassion. Though many were docile and loving souls, the holy and docile nun was mostly a myth. Just because someone put on a religious habit, did not mean the essential character of that person would or could change.

The issue of my spending too much time with Sister Carol was raised again. We shared the same work assignment in the refectory. Suddenly she was switched to the Motherhouse itself and I was sent to the laundry. We couldn't be more separated during the day. During free time we were together in a group or took a short walk and discussed our lives as novices. We discussed the 'particular friendship' concerns of the Novice Mistress, but neither of us felt any more than intellectual and emotional connection.

Days, weeks and months of learning about the vows of poverty, chastity and obedience that we would soon take and the sacred rules of the community filled us with a resolve to lead holy lives. Classes focused on learning the Carmelite Rule and what behaviors were expected and forbidden. The rules were steeped in history and not adapted to the '60s generation of new recruits. I persisted despite the inner conflict I experienced and the loneliness inherent in living such a strict life.

"We have allowed your brother to visit you," the Novice Mistress informed me one day.

Gerard waited for me in an outside sitting area. How he maneuvered to see his novice sister during non-visiting times was amazing.

"Gerard, what a surprise. How did you manage to visit me?"

"I used my Dr. Walsh voice and told them I was leaving the country soon for the army. So how is nun life?"

"It's good. It's what I want," pushing my hands further beneath my scapular.

"I'm not sure this is right. What are you trying to do?"

He leaned toward me and pointed to the watch on his hand.

"You know, when you leave this world and go to enter the pearly gates, there's not going to be anyone there. There will be no Jesus to greet you. You'll be looking at your watch and saying, where is he?"

I felt stupid sitting there in full habit, consecrated to the life he was entirely dismissing.

Could he be right?

"I don't believe that," I said.

He left after forty minutes.

My brother doesn't believe in what I'm doing with my life. He doesn't believe in God.

The laundry taught me a lot. It exposed me to much more than how to wash, fold and starch the linens to perfect stiffness. One afternoon on a cool evening, I rushed back to the laundry where I had inadvertently left my sweater.

As I opened the outer door, I heard strange sounds coming from the folding room. Flickering light reflected through the beveled glass panels on the inner door, which was open, just a sliver. Filled with curiosity, I quietly approached the opening from the adjoining wall and looked through the slit of light. My first impulse was to let out a shriek, but I stifled it. Two of my fellow novices were on top of each other in their white, regulation underpants. Two lit sacristy candles revealed their faces as their bodies slid up and down each other, grabbing and kissing, hands reaching deep between their thighs.

"You sure kiss well for a nun," one whispered with a soft chuckle to the other. Soft moaning sounds of pleasure and clandestine excitement fell onto the freshly laundered sheets, sacred linens waiting to be slept upon by bodies consecrated to God. Their habits were thrown on the folding table, abandoned in their desire for each other. I was concealed in darkness. My body was unable to move. The more I stayed, the more mesmerized I became, the more I became part of what they were doing. My own nipples began to hurt and I felt a throbbing between my legs I never felt before. Suddenly Sister Angela arched her back and cried out, "Oh my gggod, ohhh my god" convulsing her entire body. Sister Magdalene placed her hand over her mouth and whispered in her ear, "Quiet. No sounds. Quiet." My feet felt as though they were nailed to the floor. I felt the rising fever in my cheeks. Somehow I moved, slowly backing away from the light and scared to death that they would discover me, terrified by my own physical response and horrified by what I saw.

Did they think the laundry would wash away their sin?

Did they think the stain placed upon their souls would vanish?

My pace quickened as I hurried to the chapel, early for vespers, but needing the comfort, the protection, the healing of my prayers.

Oh my God! Oh my God! What am I to do? Help me to calm my feelings, to steady myself. I will keep quiet. I will never say what happened. I confess only to you.

Don't let them be caught. Help me remove what I saw from my mind. With you I can do anything. I will devote myself all the more to your love and service. Tomorrow I will re-wash all the sheets. It will be that nothing happened. I will wash the stains away.

I begin to read *Psalm 23* as the chapel filled.

The Lord is my Shepherd, I shall not want.

He leadeth me to lie down in green pastures.

He leadeth me beside still waters.

He restoreth my soul.

Each nun, novice and professed entered the chapel and took her assigned place facing the altar, hands placed beneath their scapular, heads bowed. Each was a picture of joyous resignation and self-denial. The two lovers, Sister Magdalene and Sister

Angela entered separately. Sister Angela was flushed and flew in with her headpiece slightly askew. Sister Magdalene made a particularly long genuflection before the altar, fixing her gaze at the crucified Christ, her Beloved, before taking her seat. I did not want to look but I had to witness their transformation from nakedness amid the laundry linen on the floor to full habit and the pews of the chapel.

Recreation lasted forever, as all I wanted to do was disappear to my silent cell. I did not engage with either of the sinful sisters but watched from a distance as they played the piano together and others sang along. They did this often and it always seemed so innocent, so lovely. Now I knew it was an expression of their intimacy and their love.

The convent was particularly cold that night. I quickly slid between the icy sheets, seeking a comfort and warmth that was not there. I pulled the covers up around my shivering shoulders only to be immediately transported back to the laundry room. The strong odor of sex that wafted through the door filled my nostrils as my mind flashed back to my sisters' nakedness. Their bodies anointed the newly laundered sheets.

I repeated until I fell asleep, "The Lord is my Shepherd. I shall not want."

As the two years of Novitiate training began to quickly pass, I faced the question, was this journey one I could continue to take? Shakespeare in *Twelfth Night* wrote, *No prisons are more confining than those we know not we are in.*

I prayed to God for help in knowing what to do. I stared at the tabernacle that contained His body and blood and at my crucified Jesus high on the cross.

Silence. Only silence. Celestial silence. Carmelite silence.

Was God revealing himself to me in the silence? The answer I heard in the gentle breeze from the chapel window was that I was not suited for religious life.

I renounced the transformation required by the convent. I wanted a life of dedication to make a difference but not at the expense of surrendering my deepest beliefs. The purpose was to erase the individual spark within. I came into more conflict with my superiors on a regular basis, mostly about minor infractions. Everyone had to agree with this illusion in order to give credibility to the quest, to prove that it exists. Deep down there had to be doubters and disbelievers, but everyone basically believed that everyone believed. The line between reality and delusions grew thinner and thinner. My plans, my dreams of being a nun grew darker. My world was falling apart. My heart felt like it was breaking into pieces like the sudden shattering of a stained glass window.

I grabbed a moment of conversation with Sister Carol.

"I've decided to leave. It's clear that I am not happy and it's only a matter of time before being asked to leave."

"I've come to the same conclusion. I can't accept the traditional thinking any longer," she said. "What will you do?"

"My sister went to nursing school in England and they loved her. I'm sure I would be accepted. They give you room and board and a small stipend while you get a nursing degree. I need to get away from everything . . . from nuns in particular."

The following day she asked, "Do you think I could go to England with you?"

"Why not? We'll both apply."

We wrote letters to the Director of Nursing at Worcester Memorial Hospital, telling her of our desire to study in England. Sister Carol snuck our letters in the middle of the outgoing mail left on a table in the front hall of the Motherhouse.

I wrote a letter to the Novice Mistress and told her I had decided to leave. I don't remember speaking to her. The very sad memory is that no one in authority in the Novitiate took the time to have a conversation with either of us. The plans were made quietly for our departure and we waited separately, like prisoners for release. No goodbyes. No nothing. It just wasn't done.

The night before I left, I had a disturbing but awesome dream.

My cell was consumed by fire. It broke into fragments. The walls collided. I raced through a door into an adjacent room that was full of water that led to yet another room also full of moving water. Endless rooms opened up on each other. I swam forward, through the doors, through water and fire.

In the morning the dream reinforced my decision to leave. I could not go through the motions of compliance any longer, and so my place was empty in the Chapel . . . a statement to the community, to God, to myself. I sat on a bench overlooking the Hudson River when an elderly professed nun I did not know approached me.

"Sister, you will be leaving in an hour. Your clothes are in your cell for you to change. Leave everything on the bed. Come to the front of the Motherhouse. You will be driven to the bus station to go to New York City. Your family will meet you there."

She rushed off without another word.

I put one foot in front of the other in a blur, a daze. This was it. It was over.

My old clothes were in my cell. The clothing ritual from Reception Day rewound like an old black and white film.

Carefully, I removed my white veil and placed the straight pins on the desk. I lifted the scapular that hid my hands over my head. The white neckband and chest piece fell to the floor. My head was uncovered by pulling the hood that enclosed it forward, leaving my extra short hair plastered to my scalp. The heavy tunic reluctantly untangled itself from my young body. My identity as a novice fell off. I no longer belonged. My favorite blue dress waited for me. I recognized it. What would it look like on me now? The dress felt light against my body and tighter, filling the outline of my breasts. It stopped at my knees. The shoes hurt. But it was like wearing nothing. Naked without my religious clothes, I passed through the front door to re-enter the outside world. The Novice Mistress and another senior nun, Mother Giles, drove down the long roadway to the entrance gate, onto the busy roads to the local bus station. There was complete silence except for the sounds of passing cars and my crying in the back seat. Even though I made the decision to leave, I was distraught. Frightened. Lost. The Novice Mistress did not say a word the entire ride.

Mother Giles turned to me and said the only words that were spoken, "Just remember that this is another step in your life. You will be okay."

I will never forget her kindness by speaking those words to me. Thank you. That is what holiness can be.

Chapter 11

Spiritually and emotionally stripped naked, I stepped back into the world, uncertain about my beliefs, my goals, and my future. I had to start all over. The whole world felt upside down and unpredictable. Betrayed by beliefs that were instilled from a very early age by nuns, priests, and my family background in Ireland and in the US. Betrayed by my own blind acceptance. There was nothing but a deep sense of disillusionment, of loss and mistrust.

Who am I?

I found that the answer to life's challenges was not going to come from outside, from institutional ideologies, but from within me. Who was my true self? I followed a script I thought was real. Not. Not real. Not right for me.

Fortunately, I had not lost my true self forever. I was young and could learn how to re-interpret life and find my way. I could learn to live consciously. Blind compliance with ancient traditions was finished. Quite ironically, the convent gave me freedom and courage to question conventional thinking and continue the journey. I acquired strength to know that I could choose to be out of step with the world and survive.

I went home to the safety of family. As parents do, my parents were immediately swept up into this passage in my life. Both were reeling from my sudden return and worried about my future. Dad was quietly relieved that the convent was not permanent. Mom had more issues understanding what had occurred and was a little disappointed, though she never said so. I was not much help in lessening their fears.

Within two weeks, Karen, formerly Sister Carol, and I each received a letter from England saying they would love to have us as students in the fall.

England afforded the perfect escape from the familiar. At that point in life, it was exciting. A new beginning. Grainne had graduated from the nursing school there and we had relatives in Bath.

Within a few months of leaving the convent, the Worcester Royal Infirmary Nurses Residence became our new home. It was still an institution with rules and schedules and a 'learn while you're doing' approach to nursing education. But we had an independence and freedom to explore the world in our twenties. The best was the ease of flying to the rest of Europe on holidays or long weekends, staying in Youth Hostels in Paris, Amsterdam, and Rome. The pubs were the center of the social scene in England and many a night we had to ring the Night Supervisor to let us in since we were past curfew. Some evenings we would climb the side of the building up the waterspouts to get in through a pre-opened window. We ended up in the Director of Nursing Office one day for a lecture on the risks of pregnancy.

"I am very disturbed about both of you staying out past curfew hours. Your sister was such a model nurse, I am disappointed you are not like her."

Hello, did you forget we were just set loose from a convent? Yes, we are discovering the world on your turf but we have to.

Grainne had resigned from the Art Students League in New York City to study nursing. She brought her love for painting and drawing with her and created a line of animals from *Winnie the Pooh* that hung from the hallway entrance to the children's unit at the main hospital. They included a soft brown teddy bear along with a kangaroo, a rabbit, a little pig and a bouncing tiger.

The Director of Nursing was a fat woman with a Worcestershire accent that dropped her 'Rs'. So "sister" would sound like "sistaa." The rays from the morning sun highlighted the hairs on her chin. Most amusing was her propensity to reach each arm over her large body and in succession scratch the opposite armpit while lecturing about proper behavior expected of a nurse.

It was hard to take her seriously. Not that we would have anyway.

In a nutshell, I hated England. It was what you refer to in relationships as a rebound relationship . . . not going to last, but gets you to the next level. England had solid hands-on training in nursing though it was too lacking in theory and academics for my taste. The men I dated were unimpressive except for Mario in Rome. He and I hung out for three days. Karen and I remained good friends. I made plans to return home.

My story would not be honest if I did not say that I had thoughts about re-entering the convent. Nothing moved me in life. Perhaps I was running away from the world and back to a familiar place. I convinced myself that I had made a mistake in leaving the convent and re-applied. I was accepted back, except to wait one year. I waited.

My English nursing education was cut in half when I returned home with the intention of re-joining the Carmelite Order. People thought I had lost my mind. I believe I had.

My nun bags were half packed again when I paid a visit to the convent in New York City where I volunteered in high school. During a pleasant conversation with the Superior of the House in her spacious office, I had a Joyceian epiphany. This is a gestalt moment when suddenly a self-realization occurs and you see clearly what is at the end of the fork.

A young newly-professed nun knocked on the door and entered the room. She apologized for the interruption. Enclosed in full habit, her tiny hands wrung nervously as she scanned the room and fixed her attention on her superior behind the desk. She spoke.

"Mother, may I have permission to buy three pairs of new underwear?"

The intimacy of the request alarmed me, but even more so, that she had no qualms about asking in front of me. Humiliation hung in the air. Only I felt the embarrassment, the willing debasement.

"You can purchase them. You remember Maeve from the Novitiate. She's rejoining us."

A saintly smile crossed her face. "Oh yes. You were the reader at meals who put Jesus on the cross."

I smiled, pleased that she remembered my reading. She left bowing to both of us, grateful for having her request granted. Breakthrough to sudden, immediate insight.

This is the daily life I will be accepting. No. No. I can't.

"Goodbye, Mother. I have to leave," I said.

I opened the heavy iron front door of the building to the vibrant streets of New York. The loud click of the lock behind me signaled the final closure of this phase of my life. I knew I could not go back to my silent cell ever again.

"Mom, Dad, I decided I'm not going back to the convent."

"What? When did that happen?" they asked. "We think you should finish your training in England."

I responded, "I can't go back there either."

Stalemate.

What will I do? I haven't finished anything. Will I ever finish anything?

An older family friend took me out to dinner for a talk. Seamus advised that I follow what I wanted to do and not worry about what people were saying I should do. We talked about life not being a straight line. Exploring side roads was part of the journey. He advised me to trust myself.

"No one can give you the answers. They are within you."

I was a mess. I took his words to heart. After dinner we went to see a local production of *The Seagull* by Anton Chekov.

Dissatisfaction with oneself is one of the fundamental qualities of every true talent was written on the inside of the cover of the playbill.

Seamus could never have planned how truly suitable this play was, following our conversation. This tragicomedy opened with Masha answering the question of why she wears black all the time.

I am mourning for my life.

The characters created their own misery rather than pursue their dreams and their authentic selves. These people stayed in my mind and heart.

Maybe there is something I should change, like completing what I start and learning to be more aware of my choices?

I became determined to set my life on the right course. Hunter College, part of the City University System of New York at 68th Street and Lexington Avenue became my new learning ground. I promised myself that I would complete the four-year program earning a bachelor's degree in Nursing with honors. My academic schedule was packed with liberal arts and science courses, opening my mind to new ideas.

My family, society and the Church had already written my life script. I walked into my own, one entirely different and even opposite. It felt as though just about everyone was way over there on one side, and I, along with the new people I encountered, on the other.

First, you don't tell anyone. You lead an alternate and parallel existence. You open doors and enter, not knowing what to expect, but still compelled to go there. You have to. You have no choice, if you are going to follow the deepest urges to be yourself.

Dreams reoccurred with powerful messages. Unconscious nighttime encounters left me confused and frightened. They were decent enough people in my dream.

I go over the edge, indulging in the most passionate of forbidden love. It feels so real. I lose all sense of balance. Restraint doesn't occur to me.

At first, sleep alone brought these images. Scary. Why was this happening? The images intruded into my daytime thoughts and demanded recognition. They demanded action. I remembered the warning of 'particular friendship' from the convent but overwhelmingly felt drawn to women, especially to what were known as androgynous women.

I flashed back to the erotic laundry scene of the two novices and to my own aroused reaction. I internalized the same homophobic ideas taught by the church and believed in by my family and the majority. Gay liberation was in its infancy.

I began reading feminist, political writers like the poet Adrienne Rich, and Audre Lorde, who attended Hunter College. They gave me words and brought my understanding about racism and sexism to the surface. I could not identify one gay person that I knew. There was no Internet at that time. There was no one safe to talk to about my feelings. I researched gay organizations in the Yellow Pages and came up with The Daughters of Bilitis. This was the first Lesbian political organization founded in 1955 to support the growing gay rights movement. Bilitis was a fictional character said to have lived on the island of Lesbos with Sappho. I called to talk to someone.

"Hello. I'm trying to find out information . . . I'm having thoughts that I might be gay and don't know what to do or where to go."

A voice answered, "Just because you're having feelings, does not mean you have to act on them."

Silence . . . Confused, I responded, "Oh, Okay. Thanks," and hung up.

Did they know who I was? I think they must have known. How could I have called a complete stranger? I'll never do that again. I must be losing it.

This was not what I expected. Obviously, I did not reach a very liberated or 'out person' on the phone that day. Additionally, they did not have training in place for calls such as mine, which seems a little odd. It was the '70s in New York City and I was lost, shamed, embarrassed. I may as well have been on a remote, homophobic, undiscovered island. It stopped all action on my part for six months and threw me to the very back of the proverbial closet.

The dreams continued, disconcerting and enjoyable at the same time. Fortunately, I immersed myself in the most outrageous literature course at Hunter College, reading and studying Proust's *Remembrance of Things Past*, James Joyce's *Ulysses* and Hermann Hesse's *Demian.*

On the home front Dad decided to throw a house party for the women in his office and asked if I would help. Sometimes things happen for a reason.

"Of course I will help," I said.

Eight women came and we had a fun afternoon. I joined in the conversations and was totally struck by one woman in the group. She was vibrant and strong in her late thirties and gave me an intense feeling of someone different. She lived in Manhattan and asked me if I wanted a lift back to Bellevue Hospital where I was living in the dorms. I jumped at it, excited like I hadn't been in a long time. Conversation was light but I knew she held an answer for me.

"So, Dad . . . Deborah was a lot of fun. What do you think about her?" I asked on my next visit home.

"She is great fun, but I think she has lavender in her blood."

What did he just say? I knew and did not know at the same time.

The knowing was enough for me to pursue a plan to get in touch with her again. Dad's address book held her address and I wrote her a letter. It was risky, considering she worked with my father. I wasn't telling him I was getting in touch with her, but I had no other option at the time.

Dear Deborah,

I met you at my dad's party a few weeks ago. This is Jim's daughter, Maeve. You may remember driving me back to Manhattan.

I'm writing to you after secretly getting your address from my Dad's book. Please do not be alarmed by my letter. I know it is out of the ordinary. After meeting you, I thought you might be someone with whom I could discuss something that has been disturbing me. Would it be possible to meet for dinner one evening when we could talk? You can respond to me at home.

Thanks in advance.

Sincerely,

Maeve

This was desperation and determination in action. I had to follow this one lead that could help me with real information. I was terrified mailing the letter and equally terrified waiting for a response.

Will she mention to my father that I wrote to her or will she know not to say anything?

Her answer was "yes" with a time and place, Donovan's Pub, a fixture in Woodside, Queens, right across the street from Saint Sebastian's Church where I went to grammar school. Half way through the tasty, juicy bacon cheeseburger, I revealed my angst about being gay.

"I thought that's what you wanted to talk about," she said. "My partner and I can bring you to a gay bar in the City if you would like and we'll introduce you to the gay world."

Thrilling, thrilling, relief in sight at last. I can't believe I did this. She knew not to say anything to Dad.

"Yes. When? Where?" I couldn't wait.

It was my birthday. Maybe you don't remember actually being born, but you do remember being born to new experiences. We remember our first date, first job, first airplane ride, first time we tasted escargot, fried frog's legs, oysters or some other exotic food, first time we were devastated by a failed relationship. A new baptism waited. I was about to enter a lesbian bar for the first time on my 25th birthday.

Chapter 12

Gianni's was located on dark and deserted 19th Street between 6th and 7th Avenue. Deborah and Alice were dressed as though they came straight from work. Deborah wore a grey business pantsuit and Alice, a more casual look, with sweater and corduroy pants. I stood behind them as they knocked on the door with familiarity and ease. A small window opened to view the customer. I thought they gave a secret password as you would getting into a speakeasy, or was that just my imagination? Rosebud perhaps?

This has to be the scariest thing I have ever done. Oh my god. Am I crazy?

The door opened and we entered a gloomy interior with a full bar to the right. People danced in the back of the room. Music pounded the smoky air. Music of the '70s. Disco, from

Donna Summers to The Village People. Glasses clinked at the bar as people leaned into each other, deep in conversation. A few turned to witness the newcomers to the already packed room. Most were white women from different backgrounds and ages. Deborah ordered me a gin and tonic and I settled in with my back to the wall. I looked at the dance floor like a sociologist visiting a new island and seeing the natives for the first time. It allowed me to feel a psychological distance while I took full mental notes. Bodies moved in and out of the light by the neon beer sign on the wall, illuminating cleavage, faces, and short haircuts of some, while leaving the rest of the bodies in darkness.

I stood really still and a chill of closeted fear ran down my spine. I had never seen women dancing together, laughing, bodies close, gyrating, grinding to the music.

I can't believe this really exists. Is this for real?

Hooked on a Feelin,' a pop song by Blue Swede played with some of the women mouthing the words to each other as they danced. I heard pieces of those words shouted into the dance floor.

Hold me tight.

It's all right.

I'm high.

In love.

Believe.

They permeated the air. I took a deep breath. My lungs filled. My heart received the words.

Two young women kissed passionately in a corner table beside me. I smelled the sweet sweat and the body heat intermingled with the smoke and dankness of the dark space.

Where am I? Have I died and gone to heaven? Wait. Stop the action.

I walked over to Deborah sitting at the bar and asked, "Are there men in here? I thought only women were allowed?"

She responded, "They *are* women."

I learned about role-playing and the butch/fem. phenomenon of dressing in a male/female role. I was amazed, both attracted and repulsed by what I witnessed. I wondered where I might fit in. I didn't feel like either a butch or a fem. Turns out I could just be myself. A preppy looking woman came over and asked me to dance but I shyly declined.

"Ok, maybe next time," she said. She threw a smile over her shoulder as she headed back to her seat.

I just had to keep looking at the dance floor at that point, scared shitless. I couldn't move. I left with Deborah and Alice after about two hours.

"See you next week," the female bouncer at the door said as I exited.

I responded, "I don't think so," to which she said with confidence, "Oh, you'll be back. You'll be back."

She was right. The following Friday I had a date with a man I had been seeing for a while. He was sweet and handsome and we both shared a love for photography. During the day he was a construction worker at the World Trade Center. At dinner in a cozy downtown Italian restaurant, all I could think of was the women's bar. I feigned a headache and he took me back to the dormitory at Bellevue Hospital. Within half an hour I was inside Gianni's on my own. I couldn't stay away. I was hooked on the feeling. My need was stronger than my fear. I had found my people.

I ordered my own gin and tonic and found one of the few seats with a small table at the edge of the dance floor in a secluded corner of the dingy but all so perfect room. Scared and courageous I sat and watched. Maria the bartender gave me a quick smile as she recognized me from the week before. I abandoned my male date to take my place at the table of gay life. The transformative choice I made by returning on my own, was whether to remain in the closet or step out of the closet. It was not to live a gay life or a straight life.

These walls were a bit like the walls of the cloister. They formed a sanctuary for each woman to safely explore her identity and her own depth with her 'sisters' of like mind. Behind the bar Maria called all the shots. Androgynous, feminine, warrior-like appearance, she exemplified a classic Spanish beauty. She kept an eye on the newcomers and enforced the rules of bar etiquette and lesbian courting. She did this while she poured the drinks and socialized with her known, trusted, steady customers. I did not make the same mistake I made in the convent with the Mistress of Novices and didn't give her a salute or any gesture at all. I knew better.

The women came to find love and meaning and most importantly, self-acceptance. Inside these walls everything was normal and a respite from isolation and ignorance. Here, you let your hair down, no matter how short it was. The gay bar represented a Temple of 'particular friendships,' a haven for forbidden love. Here spirits soared and prayers were answered.

I prayed mine would be.

The music started. *Rock me gently, rock me closely.*

A woman walked to my table and said, "I'm English Dee, would you like to dance?" Before I could decline, she took me by the hand to the dance floor. She was lanky, butchy with a big smile and took command of the movements.

English Dee's main goal was to dance as close as possible.

"I'm Irish Maeve. You're a good dancer."

She was a working class type from Liverpool and spoke with strong Liverpoolian accent. Gianni's was her second home. She introduced me to a group of women and I was on the way to becoming part of the community. I was clueless about the drama going on around me with lovers and ex-lovers as well as the Mafia man at the front of the bar. He packed a gun as well as a bag of bagels and bialys "for the girls." He protected the clientele and the business.

Occasionally, Maria glanced my way as she shook a drink in the air, and gave me the feeling that she was keeping a protective eye on me. Just then two piping hot trays of pasta with marinara sauce and garlic bread appeared for everyone to eat for free. This was the routine around ten at night on the weekend. The women dived into the food and then resumed dancing and drinking until the early hours of the morning. An old woman, like a character out of a Dickens novel, moved through the crowd with a basket of red roses over her arm. A black kerchief tied beneath her chin covered her thin wisps of white hair. Her smile revealed missing and discolored teeth. She extended a red rose towards a seated couple, her bony hand covered with translucent skin, oblivious to the well-developed thorns within her grasp. She whispered to them in a barely audible voice, "A rose for your sweetheart for a dollar?" She did well in that back room.

English Dee said around 2:00 a.m. "C'mon, love. We're going to Bickford's Coffee Shop for a sip of coffee. Join us."

Later I found out this was a way to see someone in bright lights after the darkness of the bar and get to know them better. Two of the women were in their late twenties, pretty, and madly in new love. They held onto each other as though some mighty force would separate them if they let go. They were both in college and dressed in preppy style clothes. English Dee was in her forties and showed the effect of steady bar life. A cigarette balanced between her lips. She identified as a soft butch, her manly haircut, blue jeans and plaid shirt with work boots completed the sought-after effect. After eggs and coffee I cabbed it back to the dorm. "See you next week," I said as I got into the cab.

It didn't come fast enough. I felt the same giddy excitement as I knocked on Gianni's door the following Friday to meet Deborah and Alice and catch them up on my progress. An hour later English Dee came through the door directly to my barstool.

"Hey, love, 'ave you 'erd of Bonnie and Clyde's over on West 3rd Street? There's someone there that wants to meet ya."

"Who?" I answered.

"A friend of mine," she replied.

Deborah gave me a nodding smile and I took off. Bonnie & Clyde's was a hangout for politically active lesbians and a place where gay women socialized across racial and class lines. The downstairs where we first entered was again dark with a pool table and seating along the side walls. A heavy-set black woman was bent over the pool table setting up the balls. Her tight black V-neck cotton top hugged her breasts as they fell forward onto the table without obscuring her view, but providing an exceptional one for me. Nothing interfered with her aim. A loud smack was heard and the balls spread across the table in just the position she wanted. English Dee gave me a smile and a nudge forward towards a woman convulsed in laughter among a group of friends. I looked back as I saw the first shot pocketed two of the balls.

"Maeve, you're like a kid in a sweet shop. The person I want you to meet is sitting over by the wall. C'mon." she said.

"Maeve, I'd like you to meet my friend Sid."

We shook hands and Sid said, "I heard you had a close call with the convent."

"Ah, yes. How did you know that?"

She responded, "Oh, news gets around in the bars."

"So, how did you get a name like Sid?" I asked.

"That's my street name. My real one is Cindy."

Later one of Sid's Park Slope friends, an attractive Italian, told her she was interested in dancing with me. "Could you ask her to dance with me," she said to Sid. "Hell no," replied Sid. "If I'm going to ask her to dance, I'm asking her to dance with me." She did. We did. Her forward style disarmed me and we quickly got into an unending conversation about our lives.

"Let's get out of this gloomy place and go grab a bite somewhere."

Sid became my first gay date, my first love, my first partner, my first break-up, my lifelong friend and confidant, and my first introduction to Jewish culture and family life. Was I in for a ride!

Chapter 13

Luna Park in Brooklyn? I never heard of it. Where on earth is that?

I remembered Dad took us to Brooklyn to an amusement park when we first came to America. Sid lived right beside that amusement park in Coney Island. The famous Wonder Wheel filled her bedroom window, as it circled the sky. A perfect symbol to begin our new life.

We took our seats beside each other, relished in new love and readied for the ride. Sid's mother Shirley saw Luna Park as the center of the universe, and a major part of that universe was her only daughter. A shiksa (a non-Jewish female) like myself from a foreign place like Ireland did not fit into the design.

"Where did you get a name like Maeve?" she asked me one day.

"I was born in Ireland. It's Celtic," I replied.

"Oh, Irish. A Catholic. What do you want with my daughta?"

Luna Park was a self-created Jewish ghetto or shtetl. The word "shtetl" is Yiddish, and it means little town. Many families survived hatred and endured prejudice and discrimination as Jews in European towns. Some survived the holocaust. They created a sense of security in their neighborhood by surrounding themselves with only the familiar.

They clung to traditional roles for the husband, wife and children. They were quick to protect by rejecting anyone who challenged their view or went astray. Jews married Jews. Men married women. The men worked. The women talked on the benches around Luna Park, raised the children, and made good brisket. Everyone knew everyone else's business.

Shirley remarked once, "Why would anyone want to go anywhere else? We have everything right here in Coney Island."

Sid came out to her family two years before she met me. Being gay was what Shirley called a "shanda," a shameful thing, a scandal. She could not speak of it. On one visit she pointed to the painting of Sid on her sixteenth birthday hanging over the piano, hair flowing, wearing a soft white dress, and said, "This *WAS* my daughta."

She desperately loved her family on her terms; Irving, her soft spoken and quiet husband, Benny, her older, sharp witted son, Sid, courageously speaking her truth, and Stephen, the brightest and youngest, who also announced he was gay at fourteen.

Sid ran home one day full of excitement. She hoped her mother would see a way to accept her. At a Gay Pride Parade she attended, she bumped into the daughter of Shirley's best friend from Luna Park. Both mothers shared their lives on the park bench every week. They shared intimacies.

"Mom, I met Ethel Blumberg's daughter at a gay pride parade. She is gay. Why don't you talk to your friend about my being gay? It could help both of you understand."

"I will never talk about it to anyone, especially not to Ethel Blumberg," Shirley replied.

These encounters only served to make Sid stronger and determined. Sid was raised on the streets of Brooklyn and she was taking her authentic self to those same streets.

"This is who I am and I am going to live out loud, not in silence."

Her mother was tireless with suggestions for boyfriends for both of us. They always came in pairs. We sat in the small breakfast nook where everyone had to scoot in to a spot around the table.

"I have found a man for each of you. Sid, I found a nice man for you. He is a doctor. Maeve, I have a construction worker for you."

Sid and I looked at each other and nearly doubled over laughing. It was so transparent and so 'Shirley' by this point, and sadly hysterical. This nook was also the arena where uncensored opinions, disagreements and anger were served along with the bagels and cream cheese. If words could wound, this table witnessed massive bloodshed. For me it was sheer culture shock. One conversation I remember went like this:

Shirley was spitting mad at Benny. He had gotten his picture taken with a belly dancer on the boardwalk in Coney Island while on his beat as a cop. The buxom Martha Huttner was teaching a group of spirited seniors how to belly dance. One of them yelled to the boys in blue who came upon the scene, "Let's see a cop belly dance." After a little coaxing by the gathered crowd, Benny – alias Benny the Belly – with his handcuffs swaying from his belt, wiggled top and bottom with Martha. The boardwalk swayed. The crowd joined in. Gabe Pressman from NBC TV, the Daily News and the Post caught the action.

Shirley banged her stained coffee cup on the yellow formica counter top and poured another. Quickly she flicked the old silver lighter and took a deep pull on a cigarette, all in preparation for her tirade. She turned sharply to face Benny head-on in her purple housedress with a pocket that held her cigarettes, her permed red hair colored from a bottle, as her cigarette cut through the air.

"You have embarrassed your mother and your father and brought shame to the uniform. How can I leave my house with this picture all over the front pages of the newspapers? What are the neighbors thinking? I can't even look at you as my son," Shirley yelled in a staccato voice.

I froze.

"Benny, I think if you want to be a cop, you have to honor the uniform and not debase it. It goes with the job," Stephen said seriously.

Sid piped in, obviously grateful to have her mother pissed off at someone else in the family for a change,

"I think you had the chutzbah, the balls to do it. However, while you were belly dancing, what if a crime happened that you didn't see because you weren't paying attention?"

Benny took a deep breath, leaned back in his chair and responded in true Brooklynese. His cheeks inflated as each word was pronounced deliberately, with emphasis and pauses. His pudgy lips surrounded each syllable before its release into the breakfast nook.

"It seems to me each of you has a lot to say about being a cop that you know nothing about. Now, if anybody else here even had any kind of job, that might help your limited understanding . . . but you don't. This front-page picture of me, I might say, is a very good capturing of my sexy physique. It is clear to me, however that none of you have the intelligence to understand why an officer of the law, such as myself, would engage with the public in this fashion.

But I will try to explain . . . slowly so you will comprehend. It is called Public Relations. Simply mingling with the public as an officer of the law, thereby gaining their trust as a public servant . . . The everyday spectators and the lovely belly dancer, because of me, have a new respect for the law. In conclusion, I think all of you in this family should have more respect for me."

If those words were exchanged in my Irish Catholic home, nobody would ever talk to one another again.

Benny later in life became an accomplished attorney and used his oratory skills and good will to benefit many, including friends and family.

It was at this same table that I received my introduction to Yiddish. I learned that I belonged to that part of non-Jewish society referred to as the Goyim or gentiles. One of my favorite words was "alte kaker" which refers to someone old who walks "like he had shit in his pants." Sid demonstrated how this looked by walking from side to side with legs apart, and I cracked up. Another favorite was "faklempt" that means you are all mixed up.

"I can't talk now. I'm all faklempt. Talk amongst yourselves." A frenzied facial expression and flailing arms accompanied the statement. I loved learning the old Yiddish words. Like Irish idioms, they captured the essence of language.

I brought Sid home for Easter Sunday dinner early on in our relationship. It seemed only right to give equal time to the Catholic side.

"Mom, Dad, meet my new friend Sid. She's Jewish. We met in college."

I did not tell them we were dating. They embraced her, especially Dad, who loved to discuss politics with her. Mom liked her, which was saying a lot. She was more cautious than Dad. It became a given that Sid was invited to all events. She became part of my family, my mishpocheh.

Sid and I were delighted to observe little Stephen growing up blatantly gay and exceptionally brilliant. Because he was the youngest by many years, he escaped the maternal wrath and razor-edged ridicule of Shirley. At the age of ten, he was a mastermind at supermarket bargain shopping. Coupons covered the breakfast nook table and were stored in large shopping bags in his room. The family budget for food was guided by double and even triple coupon days, buying one and getting one free and planning menus around "a deal... not to be missed." This talent was particularly helpful during the Jewish holidays.

"Waldbaums has Matzo on sale between 8 a.m. and 9 a.m. and on Thursday it has a special on chopped liver. Seltzer is six for a dollar."

It's not that the Simowitzes went to temple on the High Holy Holidays, and needed to have these items for breaking fast or Shabbat dinner. They were ethnic Jews with all the trappings of their Jewishness in the refrigerator and their speech. Jade Pagoda, the local Cantonese Chinese restaurant was where they preferred to eat.

Stephen had his Bar Mitzvah and I was invited. Table Six hosted Benny, his anorexic date and the newlywed, heterosexual cousins from New Jersey who kissed between each bite. Sid and I came with gay male friends, Fred and Doug. They were handsome, very much in love and into the leather scene. They came dressed in conventional suits just for us. They were such good friends. Fred was Jewish and Douglas was Italian Catholic. To Shirley, this was a Bar Mitzvah miracle. Sid would marry Fred. I would marry Douglas.

I think it was Benny who produced the weed that was passed around the table. Amidst roars of laughter from our table, the rabbi commented, "I don't know what is going on at table six, but I hope it's kosher."

This was my first Jewish ceremony and service. On that day Stephen became a man in the Jewish culture… a wonderful, gentle, loving gay man who in later years, I looked upon as my adopted brother. Many years later in his adult years, his supermarket bargain skills advanced to card counting and casino gambling. Calls at two in the morning announced yet another win.

"I just won a royal flush. $140,000."

Pictures sent from Vegas, Biloxi and cruise ships showed the royal flush or four of a kind wins. Often we'd accompany him on comped trips when we were treated like queens. He knew when to pull away from the table and enjoy a show or scrumptious meal.

Sid and I explored the gay world together, growing up within its social, political and intellectual community. She graduated from college and began her career working for the IRS. I started my first full time job in a psychiatric hospital on the Upper East Side of New York City and quickly moved up to increased responsibilities each year. We rented our first apartment together on the Upper West Side and loved it. Sid bought a car, a bright yellow Dodge Colt and we looked like a lesbian taxi service as we sped all over town.

We gave each other strength to explore and embrace our newly discovered identities. We read the history of gay culture and the lives of individuals in literature who were gay. We devoured books like Rita Mae Brown's *Rubyfruit Jungle.* We walked down Fifth Avenue for the Gay Pride Parade with our brothers and sisters of like mind and spirit. That was thrilling and frightening, knowing anyone may recognize you from the sidelines.

We shouted, "I'm gay and I'm proud," and "We're queer, we're here. Get used to it."

This took back the negative words and like an alchemical process, transformed them into power and self-affirmation. I marched, perched on my friend Fred's shoulders who was over six feet tall, as I waved a gay flag in the air. We were all very different but we shared a common bond, a common cause. It felt good to belong, to be accepted, to be heard.

Sid and I summered in Provincetown, Massachusetts or P-Town, as it is commonly known, a gay mecca where we were at home and free to be ourselves. We bicycled the dunes, played at Herring Cove beach and walked up and down Commercial Street holding hands. We stayed in gay owned bed and breakfasts and were entertained every night by gay musicians, comedians and actors. It was surreal. We packed the small entertainment venues for entertainers like Kate Clinton, a fun loving lesbian political humorist. Gay men and women mingled at the afternoon tea dances and indulgent restaurants. The annual carnival parade was totally outrageous with floats from the local businesses and everyone out on the street, dressed up and just having fun. The town was saturated with gay people and an occasional nuclear family that ended up at the furthermost point of Massachusetts, unaware of the influx of the summer gay population. Friendly straight people arrived, who just didn't care if it was gay or straight. It was a beautiful spot ... a "live and let live place." We both felt depressed when vacations were over and we had to return to reality.

"How will we remember not to hold hands when we are on the street at home?" I asked.

"That's going to be weird. I don't know. It's so natural here," said Sid.

In our third year we decided to live in an 'open relationship.' We both could indulge our young emotional and sexual appetites, knowing we would always return home to each other. We thought we had conquered the pettiness of jealousy and our love was strong.

"After all, we don't belong to each other," we said. That was the title to a discussion group we led at the Westside Discussion Group that met monthly in the West Village.

Throughout the 1900s New York City had famous salons or gathering places in homes from Greenwich Village to Harlem. They were part of the city's social life where artists, musicians and writers gathered to hang out together. One was Mabel Dodge's famous 'Evenings' hosted at her Fifth Avenue townhouse. Political and artistic ideas were launched throughout these gatherings as well as a mixing of black and white, gay and straight, young and old. We had our own Mabel in the 1970s and her name was Ruth and her 'Evenings' were in Flatbush, Brooklyn. We weren't luminaries or known experts but she was the epitome of the grand hostess, opening her home for ideas, self-discovery and pleasure. Ruth was twenty years older than most of us, Jewish and straight. We were frequently invited, as Sid was a good friend and her former neighbor. There was always music, loads of food cooked together, tons of pot, smoked and sprinkled in the sauce and minor experimentation with cocaine. She was the joy-goddess to many and the wonderful, older, accepting, non-judgmental adult in our lives.

"Come," she said one late evening, as she led me to her bedroom. "I've always wanted to know what it's like to sleep with a woman."

Chapter 14

During this period of time, Dad was coping with a worsening cardiac condition. Medications and life style changes did little to halt its insidious progression. Mom went back to work in New York City to help make ends meet after years of being at home.

The aneurysm operation at New York Hospital also did little to resolve his chronic illness. Today's medicine would have successfully prolonged his life with a quality worthy of his spirit. Mom and Dad adaptively switched roles. He began to cook creatively and had dinner ready for her when she walked in the door. I was the lookout, and announced she had rounded the corner with a minute left to arrival.

They both did this for many years before they bought a house in Catskill, New York. It was a Dutch Colonial revival with slanted roof and arched room entrances on the ground floor, steps away from St Patrick's Church and across the street from a convent. At that time Grainne was living in the next town with her husband Michael and their young family. It seemed like the perfect plan until Michael was transferred overseas to Holland and Mom and Dad ended up in upstate New York on their own. Through the years Dad continued to write little verses and this is one he wrote to Mom while coming to terms with his illness.

The stupid little verses

That I wrote you long ago

Will soon be terminated

As words will cease to flow.

The lines were my expression

Of a love that always grew

I'd find myself so tongue-tied

If I had not known you.

I visited often on weekends and holidays. Dad loved when I arrived with friends. One time he broke into a dance on the slate tiles of the covered porch, holding a freshly picked pink hibiscus from the garden in his teeth. We helped Mom make scones and Irish soda bread, which to this day I cannot replicate. We had fun times that were easy and relaxing, though we knew Dad's time was limited.

Then I met Zeena. She burst into the intimate little bar on the Lower West Side, wearing a Japanese kimono, full of life and exuberance. Sid introduced us. Zeena was exotic and exuded a palpable sexuality. Her dark bangs framed a face that softened easily, and her red lipstick surrounded a sharp-tongued eloquence and laughing smile. A lipstick lesbian fully comfortable with her femininity and her sexuality.

She loved Barbra Streisand and had detailed albums of her entire career. Barbra's silky voice played in the background of the small pub.

"Do you hear how perfect each note is sung?" Zeena asked as she swooned in appreciation.

"I'll have a Sambucca Romano," she gestured to the bartender. " I must have it with the coffee beans on fire."

The small glass of liquor rested on the bar with three coffee beans floating on top. The bartender pulled out a lighter and set them on fire. We stared as they roasted into the liquor. In seconds the fire disappeared.

"Taste it," Zeena said as she held the glass to my lips with her glowing red fingertips.

"Oh my god. It's outrageous." Took my breath away. A new fire was ignited. Within me.

As we said "goodnight," her touch sent ripples through my nervous system. I saw in her eyes, she felt the same. We would be together.

Sid and I separated, and our love evolved into a life-long friendship. Our parting was painfully harmonious. The 'open relationship' was our way of taking care of each other and ending our monogamous relationship.

"Here, you take these books. You love them," she said.

"I want you to have the table we bought in P-town," I insisted.

Zeena and I began dating. She opened up the theater world for me. Zeena played in off, off-Broadway shows, and we also attended show after show on Broadway. I completed my Master's at New York University during which time we lived in a small townhouse in the East Village. Two fabulous gay men owned it, and it had an unusual roof garden with vegetables, enormous watermelons and all kinds of unexpected plants for a

N.Y.C. rooftop. Our favorite haunt was The Duchess, an upscale women's bar on West 4th Street and 7th Avenue. It was known as a hangout for professional women during happy hour at 5 p.m. Then we would sit in the window seats at The Buffalo Roadhouse, a few doors down, devouring mussels and white Russian cocktails, watching the West Village pass by. The area was famous for small jazz clubs, tea houses that hosted poetry readings, theatres like the one on Manetta Lane, Marie's Crisis Cafe for late night piano playing when voices filled the small room in unison and celebrities stopped by to join the singing crowd.

One Halloween party at the Duchess, I dressed as a very convincing Catholic nun and Zeena as a very convincing Lina Wertmuller whore. Arm in arm we placed second in the costume contest. Zeena was a passionate, smart and loving person who took life on full blast. It was during these early years, when I thought I would be with Zeena forever that I knew the time was approaching when I needed to 'come out' to my family. With a second woman clearly in my life, I needed to have conversations with Grainne about my being gay.

During a vacation visit home we planned brunch with her at a West Village restaurant. I was nervous, waiting for her arrival. Zeena and I practiced what I would say in whispered tones. Half an hour had gone by, and no Grainne.

She rushed in wearing jelly shoes and a bright red puffer jacket, the latest in Dutch fashion.

"Sorry I'm late. I couldn't find the place," she said, quickly scanning where she had arrived.

The waiter was annoyed because we delayed our order. He pounced on the table.

"Can I take your orders, now that everyone is finally here?" he asked in a tone only a queen could produce, glaring at Grainne.

"Oh well. I'm here now. I'd like a Long Island Iced Tea to start."

The place was abuzz, waiters flying around small tables covered in red and black patchwork design. The intention was to give this expensive restaurant a cozy appeal.

Zeena squeezed my hand under the table, acknowledging we had gotten off to a rather tense start.

"Don't worry about him," Zeena told Grainne. "He can't help the drama. He'll get over it."

He reappeared with the drinks and a better attitude.

Grainne ordered the Cordon Bleu, like Zeena, and I ordered the mussels in a tangy coconut broth with fresh ginger. The mussels opened up perfectly, swirling the aroma of the broth all around us.

"So, I want to tell you something very important," I said and took a deep breath. "I'm gay. Zeena and I are a couple."

"That's great," she said a little too readily. "I knew you were. I was waiting for you to tell me. Gerard and I talked about the possibility of your being gay."

She looked and looked at me, as though searching for some outward sign of my gayness to confirm my words. Or she was thinking about her part in the family, now that she was told.

"Have you told anyone else?"

"No. I wanted to tell you first."

She was pleased to have the revelation first.

"I know you'll need time to absorb this."

"I'm fine with it. I was just waiting for you to tell me."

Zeena and I were relieved. I had come out face to face with Grainne.

I naively took it for granted that Gerard would have a similar response. I called him.

"Hi Gerard. Zeena and I had dinner a few nights ago in the city with Grainne."

"She told me."

"She told you we had dinner?"

"Yes."

"Well, I wanted to tell you what I told her. I'm gay. Zeena is my partner."

"I know. I thought you were calling me to tell me you were going to get the magic cure."

"What do you mean, Gerard?"

Silence.

"I thought you would have more understanding and acceptance."

Silence.

"Don't say anything to Mom and Dad. They don't need it."

"I wasn't intending to with Dad sick."

Silence.

I hear the click of ice cubes and a drink taken in the background.

"I don't need any cure. There's no such thing as a cure. I thought you would be more enlightened. Where is this coming from? I don't understand."

"Try the magic cure," he said again.

"That's all you're going to say?"

Silence. Hurtful silence.

I was hurt to the core. His approval and acceptance was so important to me.

"I have to go," I said. "We'll talk again."

I told Zeena about my brother's words. "You can't let him get to you. Everyone knows the idea of a cure is crazy."

"He won't even talk to me. I didn't anticipate this from anyone in my family. He's rejecting who I am."

Chapter 15

The wound is the place where the light enters you. – Rumi

My social life became my private world as I tested the waters of acceptance and the reality of homophobia. I waged my own battle with homophobia as I had naturally internalized negative stereotypes just like everyone else. I learned over and over again that I was not alone. Gay people were everywhere.

Living with a constant recognition of being different was not new to me. Becoming a nun was definitely different. My agreement to follow vows of poverty, chastity and obedience brought accolades of praise, respect and even awe. When I came out as a gay woman, it generated fear, accusations of sin, and even emotional pathology. Neither group of responses contains truth or balanced thinking and both are far removed from reality. Nor is either based on evidence. Both support denial of personal integrity and wholeness. I was going to open that door to authenticity, slowly and deliberately.

It was during this time of transformation that Dad died. I was devastated. I took him into the hospital for emergency testing and he never left. An orderly in a white uniform whisked him off from the lobby. He looked back at me as I stood powerless to change what was happening. I threw him a kiss. The last one. I believe he knew he wouldn't see me again.

I felt I had just lost someone who was forever 'in my corner.'

He was buried in Catskill. Grainne returned from Holland for the funeral. The evening of his funeral, after everyone left, my brother Gerard asked if he could talk to me in the back yard for a moment. His car was packed and he was dressed to leave.

"Of course," I said.

Not making eye contact, he spoke these words.

"I am concerned about your gay friends coming to visit Mom in Catskill. I think that one of them might take advantage of her. I don't want them to come here anymore."

I felt my entire body tense. Somehow I gathered the presence of mind to respond.

"What are you saying?"

"I mean make a move on her."

"That's crazy talk," I said

I stood looking at him in shock at his words, at his audacity and at his horrible ignorance. A mockingbird flew to the tree beside me from his home in the thistle bush and began making loud, scolding sounds, its long tail flicking up and down.

"Crazy talk, crazy talk," it seemed to be squawking. I relaxed enough to speak.

"If anyone would take advantage of her, it would be one of your straight male friends, not one of my friends. No one I associate with would do anything like that."

How the hell could he think such a thing?

I walked away, shaken by the idiotic words from my psychiatrist brother. Zeena paced with me up and down the streets of Catskill.

"It's just patently absurd," she said as we tried to understand how he could ever arrive at such a thought. In later years I concluded it must be some unresolved Oedipal issue about Mom, in addition to his utter ignorance.

The psychiatric medical profession straightjacketed his thinking. Perhaps if he had been a bar tender or shop keeper like his father or a cop on a beat, a regular guy in a regular job, he would have behaved differently. Of course we came to Catskill more often to visit Mom, but his words wounded me.

The years passed. Mom moved to Baxter, New York, to be near Gerard and her grandchildren. Grainne and Michael returned from Holland with their two young children, John and Sara. Samantha was born within the year of their return. They bought a lovely home in Oyster Bay, Long Island. Their lives focused on schools and raising a family and living a conventional suburban lifestyle. Michael and Grainne had a strong affinity for everything Irish. They sponsored children from Northern Ireland to come to the United States for the summer, away from the turmoil in their lives at home. Michael was a family man who adored his wife and each of his children.

Then he developed terrible headaches that rendered a diagnosis of a brain tumor. Their lives were turned upside down when he died. Grainne took responsibility for everything, though she was devastated by her loss of Michael. Her focus became raising her beautiful and gifted children as a single parent and helping them comprehend the pain each one uniquely felt. The loss affected all of us. The Walsh values of survival and moving forward with life, with everything you've got, took over. The years brought little relief to the three children as they often lovingly remembered their dad.

In my home, Zeena decided she wouldn't flourish in the theatre and chose the next best profession: a lawyer. We moved to Long Island and within a year, I was hired at North Pines Psychiatric Hospital where I would be groomed to replace the existing Director of Nursing. Our involvements took us to different places. Zeena and I parted a few years later with the same emotional intensity with which we began our nine-year relationship.

My lesbian generation practiced serial monogamy. It was like being married, though Marriage Equality had not been decided. It was also like getting divorced when the breakup occurred. You got your support mostly from within the gay community as the world at large, including the families we came from, did not identify with our unions as they did those of our straight counterparts. Family often held onto the hope that you might finally get involved with a man the next time. Relationships changed and each person contributed a piece of who we became as individuals and as lesbian women. We evolved.

My next relationship lasted another nine years. It was a package deal in that my partner Margaret already had a son from a heterosexual marriage and she was raising Jacob on her own. He was seven when I entered their lives.

She was a high-energy, quick-witted kind of gal with tons of ambition. Self-consciously tall, she magnified her appearance, not by slinking down, but by standing upright, speaking the unspoken and asserting her verbal agility. The sharpness of her features was modified with careful attention to makeup and expensive clothes. She had never been with a woman before, so our relationship was a major change in her life. Jacob was at first resentful that he had to share his mother's attention and relate to another adult in his routine, particularly a woman.

One day upon returning home we found three of my sweaters with holes and rips on the bed. I was shocked. We decided it must have been the cats going crazy. It was Jacob having a rage fit.

I was not prepared for being a mother, but gradually the three of us formed a family. We were a family among other families at his school.

A teacher at a parent teacher meeting looked at me and asked, "And you are"?

Jacob answered. "Maeve is my other mother."

It was at that moment that I felt acceptance from him as well as admiration for his ability to openly define himself. Ironically, acceptance was fairly easy in the world outside of our immediate birth families, but a reason for conflict within them. I was persona-non-grata to Margaret's father who refused to meet me, and my family barely tolerated her and Jacob. We held our heads high and expected equal treatment when we attended family functions. It was difficult and painful. We had no choice except to be strong for each other, protect Jacob and hope for change. Parenting is probably the most difficult endeavor in the world, especially when raising a hyperactive child with poor school performance. Margaret and I had very different approaches. Being the non-biological mother, I was often over-ruled. We both had stressful careers and our relationship fell apart, despite trying to make it work for too long.

The psychiatric hospital where I worked was thriving. It was the time of broad based insurance reimbursement and the money was rolling in. Handsome gay male friends accompanied me to mandatory leadership dinners. I loved them for coming to those boring affairs They charmed and made jokes but anyone with half a brain knew we were both gay. We had dinners on the CEO's lawn with the kitchen staff serving lobsters and steak.

My fake date Tom and I sat at the CEO's table, next to his wife on one of these occasions. The CEO, Dr. Clysdale, was not someone you wanted to piss off. He had a commanding air of authority but likeableness beneath his academic uniform of white, button-down shirts and dark suits. His once soot black hair was sprinkled with white and combed neatly back from his receding hairline. He had piercing blue eyes set deep below his unkempt eyebrows that locked you into conversation. He was a traditionalist in his approach to psychiatry and demanded complete loyalty from his staff. It was not unheard of for him to pound his desk behind his closed office door and bellow loudly at subordinates' perceived failures. But, if he liked you, he liked you. As a sideline, he evaluated the mental fitness of potential candidates entering the convent for a religious community based on Long Island. That always fascinated me, since he was Jewish.

My date joyously cut into his two-pound lobster that squirted juice directly into Mrs. Clysdale's invitingly low-cut neckline and splashed on her coiffed and dyed red hair.

Everyone held their breath at the table, waiting for an enraged response. Tom, who was a John Travolta look alike, grabbed a napkin to blot the juice trickling down her bosom. He looked her in the eyes and said, "I don't do that to just anyone, you know."

Dr. Clysdale and his wife laughed and everyone followed suit. I was up for another promotion and breathed a sigh of relief. I got it the following week.

There were emotional costs to living in the closet. Many of my gay colleagues chose not to be 'out' at work. Professionally, if I was to succeed in the system, I knew I needed to play the silence game. I never felt my life style and sexuality had anything to do with my work performance. My reputation became undisputed and though staff that reported to me knew I was gay, it did not interfere with my professional relationships with them. On the contrary, I believe being gay helped me access and develop skills and sensibilities I otherwise might not have developed. I do regret that my need to protect myself against some contemptuous and unaccepting colleagues forced me to distance myself, perhaps more than I needed to from others.

With each promotion came new challenges and difficult situations. One of the psychiatrists frequently took the opportunity to put his hand up a female waitress' dress as she served his plate at leadership dinners. He was seated next to his wife. Complaints were made but difficult to support. That was until, as Director of Nursing, I followed up on yet another complaint by a nurse.

When the nurse asked him if he would like a chocolate chip cookie, he responded, "I'd much rather be eating you." He reached out to touch her and she moved away.

I took up the cause for the nurse involved who felt powerless and thought of quitting her job.

I assured Dr. Clysdale that "There is no doubt the MD was referring to cunnilingus." This was one of those incidents when I felt the embarrassment and powerlessness of the victim. She didn't want to face him again. The shrink was gone within a week. The shrink needed shrinking.

In the years that followed, I broke through the glass ceiling for nursing and became Vice President for Patient Care Services. This gave me responsibility for all clinical disciplines from an administrative perspective. I loved the daily challenges of providing quality care and contributing to a more progressive organization.

"Do what is right for the patient" is a value we held dearly and it served to resolve many a dispute.

It truly was the discipline of nursing that kept the organization together. Psychiatrists did their rounds in the early morning, changed medication orders based on nursing reports and then retreated to their private practices. Yes, the interdisciplinary team was the key to the patients' treatment, but the nursing staff were present all the time. They gave of their compassion, implemented interventions, and many times risked their own personal safety for the safety of the patient.

Blatant homophobia asserted itself once again through Gerard. Years had passed and I was feeling that I needed to have honesty and openness with Mom about my gay life. I really thought she knew already but the conversation was necessary. I told Grainne, "I'm going to talk to Mom when I visit her this week. It's really time." The night before I left, the phone rang and it was Gerard.

"I understand you are going to tell Mom you are gay. I don't want you to tell her. It will upset her too much." A different kind of silence requested. Stifling silence. Controlling silence. Though taken by surprise, I was emotionally ready.

"I'm afraid that my relationship with my mother is totally separate from you. If I want to have a conversation with her, that's my decision, my business, not yours."

I did tell Mom, just the two of us speaking together.

Mom was demonstrating how to make Irish soda bread for the hundredth time. It was done.We slid the tray from the oven, piping hot, her apron sprinkled with the flour. It had to cool for few minutes before we cut into it. As it cooled the aroma permeated her small apartment. It smelled like Ireland. She sat on her floral winged back chair in her living room, tea in hand next to the stained glass lamp I made for her. I was on the blue couch. The butter melted instantly on the bread along with the raspberry jam.

I was terrified. My heart pounded so hard I thought it might come out of my chest. The sudden silence informed her that her unpredictable youngest daughter was about to say something heavy.

My mind flashed back to a statement she made about a year ago.

"I wish parents would allow their children to be who they are, instead of trying to change them."

At the time I interpreted this to mean that she was telling me it was okay to be gay.

It's now or never.

"Mom, I'm gay.

"We should have stayed in Ireland," she said.

"Mom, there are gay people in Ireland."

We looked at each other and I could see fear and struggle along with love in her eyes.

"How did this happen?"

"Nothing happened, Mom. It's who I am. You did nothing wrong."

"It's against the church's teaching."

"I know. But the Bible also says, *Judge not that you may not be judged, for with what judgment you judge, you shall be judged.*"

I said it quickly.

She threw me one of her stern looks. It softened as we sat.

"I wanted to be real with you, to be honest."

She wished it was different, but she was in no way rejecting or overcome by my speaking with her. She asked me some questions and I answered her concerns. It was a critical conversation that gave both of us the freedom to be real as mother and daughter. She was afraid for my welfare, my safety, my future as any good parent would be. It was a learning process for both of us. It brought us closer.

They say truth is stranger than fiction. About fifteen years later I had a gay acquaintance that lived hours from me in the Hamptons. We would communicate mostly by email and phone. One day while visiting her mom in Baxter she happened to mention my name as a gay woman she knew. Jeanette said to her daughter, "Wait a second. Did you say Maeve Walsh and she lives on Long Island and works in a psychiatric hospital?"

"Yes," replied Angela. "What are you thinking?"

"Well, Bridget Walsh across the hall has a daughter named Maeve who lives on Long Island and is an administrator in a psychiatric hospital. You know Bridget's daughter?"

These two women walked to Mass together and went shopping together each week for years. She told Mom that Angela and I were friends. Mom told me the story.

In future conversations Mom made it clear to me that I was her daughter and she would always love me. She even took it further one time when she asked if she could advise me about my partner: "I don't think you should have corrected her at dinner last night. If you did that to me, I would be upset about it." That piece of advice was one of the biggest gifts she could have ever given to me.

It is important to speak about and remember the moments of attempted control and contempt by others because of being gay. It is important because those of us who are gay have all experienced this in one way or another. We remember those moments when it happened within our family, our schools and houses of worship or places of employment. Passing on our stories to others gives hope and strength. We have come a long way towards equality. Catholic Ireland passed the Marriage Equality Law and the United States followed shortly afterwards. I never dreamed that I would witness this in my lifetime. I was so proud of Ireland and then elated when the Supreme Court decision happened at home. I bawled like a baby, twice. Change happens when people keep fighting for justice. It is important to remember, because although we have come far, people in other parts of the world still get imprisoned and executed for being gay. Facades of niceness and acceptance have fooled many

227

others, only to learn later that homophobia was right beneath the surface.

Use of the word "homophobia" was not as understood as it is today. Through my years of working in the mental health field, I would come to see "homophobia" itself as the illness. It was as destructive for those who expressed themselves in this limited way as it was for those receiving it. I was fortunate because I was strong and I had intelligent and strong friends and partners. Through the years I have heard horror stories of families disowning their gay children.

It is equally important to remember those family members and others who supported you or at least did not add to the pain of rejection.

Grainne, after a trying morning visiting in Baxter said, "Let's go to the gay parade that's happening here tomorrow. I think you need it."

I remember a CEO who was placing great trust in me and I decided I needed to tell her directly that I was gay so she would be fully informed.

Her response was, "I thought that was what you were going to say. Not a problem for me." And without skipping a beat said, "Let's talk about your plans for the new psychiatric unit we're opening in a few months."

Many times people already knew or revealed, when I was open with them, that they also were gay or their mother, sister, brother, cousin, grandmother, son, roommate, best friend was gay.

Negative words and actions are aimed at having you question your inner strength, your own knowing. Ultimately they are aimed at keeping you in the closet and in silence.

This was not going to be my future.

Metaphorically speaking, closets are stifling and confining. They have little light. They are designed to keep things neat and tidy. There is no place to move about. When closed for a long time, they smell and mildew and rot. There is no dialogue. Sometimes they have been locked so long that prying them open takes tremendous strength. Psychologically they have a deadening effect on a person's soul. Closed closets, with the right support, can be opened wide and the result is totally awesome.

Life continued to surprise and throw me curves.

The biggest one was about to knock me over. Leave me for dead.

Chapter 16

In my late forties, I spent most of my time with friends and absorbed in work. A new CEO came from Texas and brought in staff she worked with or mentored. One of these was a woman seventeen years younger than I.

"Oh, you're Maeve," she said, upon meeting me.

"Yeah?"

"I've just heard so much about you."

Georgia was a true Southern gal, with feminine charms and wiles I wasn't used to. She'd pop her head into my office unexpectedly to ask a question, her Texan accent an excuse for teasing. This was followed up with social chat about New York and what to do on Long Island. She was high heeled and lipsticked, her full form dressed for a professional look in suits, set off with bangles on her wrists and pearls around her neck.

"What are you doing this weekend?" she asked after a long day at work.

I was delighted to spend time with her, but never imagined she was gay.

On a perfect Indian summer day in October we drove to the Hamptons and took our shoes off to walk on the sand and touch the water's edge. She brushed against me. Deliberately.

"What's wrong?" she said, as she looked back.

My knees buckled.

She was living in a dump apartment, as it was all she could afford. I had a rented house on a pond, and she moved in six months later.

"What would you think if I said I wanted to go to law school?" she asked as we were driving one day.

By that time I was a goner. If it was what she wanted, then it was okay.

"You know that can put an awful strain on a relationship," I said.

"That won't happen. I can handle it."

She was accepted into a local law school and excelled. I supported her at home.

I experienced the wetlands of Texas and Louisiana in summertime. We attended a Cajun party on a bayou or swamp near where her father grew up. Two barges were tied together. One for the dance floor and one for the food. We ate steamed crayfish on newspapers sitting on the floor with our bare feet dangling in the water, moving to the sound of the squeeze-box accordion and triangle played by the locals.

She was introduced to Northern New York in the snow. My family embraced her. We had a fun Easter in Baxter, right before her semester exams. While the roasted leg of lamb cooked, we dyed and decorated eggs at the kitchen table with my nieces. Gerard even liked to talk to her. She charmed him with her stories and expressions and how she felt overwhelmed by the pace of New York City.

"When I first came here, I was nervous as a long tail cat in a room full of rockin' chairs."

With the end of law school in sight, Georgia Beau and I decided to buy the perfect home together. We walked through twenty-six places in the area we loved and found one on top of a hill, surrounded by trees. It had a water view if you craned your neck out two of the second story windows. Friends celebrated with us. We worked through the money for a down payment. I borrowed from my 401K. She was graduating from law school, so even though it was a bit beyond our current means, we wanted it. It was just plain perfect.

We closed on a Friday afternoon. The following Monday morning was cold with high winds. The furnace made a house-shaking noise when I raised the heat a few degrees to keep us warm.

"Did you hear that scary noise, Georgia?" I yelled to the other room.

Georgia Beau came into our enormous bathroom where I was getting ready for work.

Her makeup on. Hair in place.

"I'm leaving. I'm going somewhere else."

Boxes of our possessions were unopened all around. Stunned, I looked at her, dressed for work.

"What? What are you saying?"

She never changed her expression. Cold like a meat freezer. She had already moved on.

I was dumped.

"We . . . we just bought our house two days ago. Our dream house. I don't understand. What's wrong?"

"Toby and I decided it was better to go through with the sale of the house. We'd lose the money if we pulled out. You'll have the house. I want to be with her."

"You're moving in with her? When did this happen? You said you needed a friend. You said if something happened to me, you'd have no one in New York. Oh God! I . . . I . . . Oh God."

No response. Silence.

"Let's talk about this. You can't be serious."

"I'll be late for work," she said.

The front door closed behind her. She pulled out of the driveway. She left for work.

I slumped to the floor unable to get a thought straight. I couldn't remember my best friend's number. I called Steven at 7 a.m. hysterically crying.

"Hello," he answered still asleep.

"Georgia is leaving me. I can't remember Sid's number. I can't find it. I can't think."

"Try to slow down. I can't believe it. You just moved in, didn't you?"

"Yes. We're still unpacking."

"Here's Sid's number. I'll call you back."

The pain began to spread. I couldn't see. Tears and disbelief comingled. I dialed the phone.

"What's wrong? You never call me at this time."

"She . . . she's moving in with her career counselor from law school. I thought this was it . . . this was my life relationship . . . I'm standing here in the middle of our new home. We just bought this together."

"Did something happen?"

"No . . . I don't know . . . nothing."

"Try to do what you have to the next few hours. I will get you a ticket to come to California. Get time off from work," Sid said in obvious disbelief.

"Nobody breaks up like this," she said in anger.

I drove to work barely able to see the road. Tears streamed down my face. Non-stop. Non-stop crying. This was brutal. I never saw it coming. I never detected she was only making the motions of intimacy, that building a future together was a facade, a fake, a lie.

Sid gathered me from the plane. We talked and talked. I couldn't stop crying.

I saw a therapist friend of hers for a long session.

"I can't believe this is true," I kept saying.

She helped me get a grip just for the next few weeks. She applied emotional band-aids.

Nobody could believe it. Nobody who knew us together could believe it. Being gay didn't feel very happy now. There was nothing gay about it. I left California after a week, temporarily pieced back together. Tentatively held in place.

Gerard called. "Mom called to tell me what happened. She compromised you emotionally and financially. We had plane tickets to come for her graduation party. We're coming anyway."

As Mom said, "She fooled us all. I can see why you didn't have a clue."

It was a shock to have him call like that. All of my family came to my side. They had finally accepted a woman in my life. Accepted me.

Benny, now an accomplished attorney, called Georgia Beau. "You know you have committed fraud with inducement, signing the closing papers to the house. The Dean of the Law School is my friend of many years. Get ready to be sued. Get ready not to graduate."

Grainne was with me when Georgia came to pick up her stuff. A male acquaintance from law school came with her. She flew through the house grabbing things, stuffing them in garbage bags as he helped carry lamps and artwork. I was crazed watching her.

"Shit happens," he said to me as he put bags in her car.

"What a cold bitch. She never even said hello to me. Maeve, you can't let her get to you. Let her go. You did nothing wrong," Grainne said.

But I did do something wrong. I didn't see what was happening. I catered to her. I didn't take care of my needs. How could I not have known these five years? What's wrong with me?

The therapist I dragged myself to was Deborah. She was not a touchy feely sort but a direct and reality-in-your-face type.

"You've been brutally betrayed. What we must figure out is how someone barreled their way into your life and left you like this. I don't see your anger. Where is it?"

"I don't know. I loved her."

"She revealed herself along the way. You didn't want to see it. Can you recall any time she did?"

"One day I asked Georgia to talk about a traumatic event she alluded to in her earlier life."

"It's too personal to talk about," she said.

"But isn't that what you do with a partner?" I replied.

Silence. I figured she'd tell me when she was ready.

"I was so blind. She revealed her dis-connection but I did not believe it."

I sat still as a stone, a sobbing stone. For days and weeks, I went through the motions of living. Work. Therapy. Home. One day after a long weekend, I woke and realized I had been wearing the same exact clothes all weekend. The bottle of wine I opened the evening before was finished. Now I was beginning to feel pissed at everything. Pissed at her. I jumped in my Buick Riviera to go to therapy and scraped the entire left side of the car backing out of my driveway too fast.

Deborah convinced me to start group therapy. I had no desire to sit with a group of strangers and pour my heart out. What would they know to help me?

The therapy room lacked anything you could call furniture and the walls were blank, except for two inspirational posters in black plastic frames. The words of Carl Jung were consoling . . . *There is no light without shadow and no wholeness without imperfection.*

Good, because I'm pretty damn imperfect.

I sat on a beat up beige office folding chair in a circle, quietly listening to others speak their stories. I didn't say a word. I found myself staring at the floor, and taking sneak looks at the clock. I couldn't wait to get out of there.

Who are these people? We have nothing in common.

My therapy group, an unlikely gathering of eight, included a teacher, an unemployed gay man, a wife who hated her husband but couldn't leave, a twenty-year-old who couldn't control her eating, a biker who just survived a road accident but his girlfriend didn't, a self effacing writer of horror fiction, a therapist in training and me.

The next week I went back for more. Clearly I needed help.

The therapist began the group. "Who would like to begin talking today?"

Before anyone could begin, the burly built guy in his thirties with a beard you could build a nest in, wearing a Harley Davidson biker vest, looked straight at me and said, "Hey lady, I want to know why you're here. Everybody talks here."

That was the start of my dialogue with my therapy group. I spoke of my pain, my fears, and my uncertainties about the future in the weeks and months that followed. Strangers I would not have shared intimate information with in the past, listened. What I found in the most unlikely of them was honesty and feedback that began my healing. I connected to them. They were wise. Compassionate. I experienced that even though they were all very different, they could help me and I them. Though I got in touch with my anger, I told Benny to halt the legal action. I just needed to get my own act together.

It was Mom who made the analogy of moving on and not allowing a failure to direct your future. One morning while sitting in my sun-filled family room after breakfast, we talked about what had happened. She sat on my beige cotton couch, fully dressed as always, her white hair neatly combed. Classy. Today her pleated skirt fell just below her knees to her nylon stockings and black small-heeled shoes. A plum colored sweater matched, and a scarf of flowers hung freely around her neck.

"We learned growing up that if a crop failed in Ireland, you re-planted or changed the crop. What else is there to do?" she said lovingly.

I began to feel strong. Changed. Alive with a new resolve to not lose sight of reality. Still, after more than a year, I could not envision trusting someone else and trusting myself. It was another beginning, but just that, a beginning, and another movement along the rhythm of life.

Chapter 17

I flew to Laguna Beach to visit Sid and escape the New York winter cold. She met me with open arms at the airport in her white shorts and Hawaiian shirt. We headed for our favorite outdoor lunch place at the Laguna Hotel overlooking the Pacific Ocean. I stood looking at the ocean waves, surrounded by bright red zinnia and sea lavender flowers in full bloom. I took a deep breath. People sunbathing on the beach made me want to run into the water and fall into the sand. I felt relaxed and invigorated.

"Hey kiddo," said Sid. "Don't you think it's about time to get back into the swing of things and begin meeting people again?"

"Nope," I replied. "I'm too old. I'm fifty-two. You can't force these things to happen."

Sid persisted. "You gotta act. It's not going to just happen. There's a new lesbian Internet matchmaking site called *Planet Out*. We're getting you signed up while you're here."

"That seems strange. Terrifying. Desperate. I don't know."

"It's the latest thing," she said.

I could sit in my pajamas, if I wanted, instead of getting all dressed up to go out on the town in hopes of a magical evening.

"Would you walk into your library at home and randomly pull a book off a shelf when you're looking for a specific book, like on the Times Best Seller List?"

She continued. "No, you'd look it up in the card catalog and then find it in the right section. The Internet does the initial screen for dating."

I decided to exchange the clink of the glasses in a gay bar to the click of the mouse on my desktop. Some fine Napa Valley chardonnay eased my anxiety as Sid and I created my profile. The picture was the riskiest aspect, presenting myself in one moment in time.

"How about this one of me wearing a funny hat with my friend Tom?"

"It could be a turnoff posing with a guy on a lesbian dating site," Sid said

"True, but I don't want to be with someone who'd be turned off."

"Go for it."

Meanwhile in a place far, far away on Long Island, another gay woman came home with her first desktop computer, expressly bought for the purpose of finding a mate. RJ, her male friend, convinced her to use technology to her personal love benefit. Together they assembled the computer and she headed for *Planet Out*.

We both answered questions like:

What is your idea of a perfect date?

What are you passionate about?

Do you have tattoos?

Do you have dogs or cats?

How important is religion to you?

What do you do to relax?

What is your favorite movie?

Both of our profiles were dispatched to Cyber-space with the same intentions that occupied the heart and mind of a suitor two hundred years ago, hoping to initiate a lady's courtship. In that letter, those carefully composed words might have revealed a declaration of love or a request to pay a visit at her home. The reader was moved by the choice of words, the script and signature, the quality of the paper and perhaps a smell that emitted when the sealed envelope was opened. A tear mark or a doodle might further reveal the writer's personality and emotions.

The World Wide Web is an unknown silent world of words and dots, connected by electrons and magnetic fields that sort and match and make introductions through a *'you've got mail'* notice. We both awaited a real response from this unknown and foreign world.

Within a week my web site was popping with potential suitors.

Which ones do I answer?

Someone around my own age. A person who understood getting hurt in a relationship but was a survivor. Honest. Real. Willing to travel and have new adventures. Cares about family and friends. A financial equal. Comfortable being gay.

With that in mind, I began the search. A few were easy to rule out. One claimed she could "communicate with the dead." While it might be a fun thing to try on a rainy Saturday afternoon, I hardly wanted to team up with a wacko who actually believed she could do this.

Another was a Hungarian psychiatrist who entered the United States illegally. Her tall body pranced into the small coffee shop with an air of importance. She was dressed in Gucci boots, pressed blue linen pants, fluffy silk shirt and a Hermes of Paris scarf with the designer's name cascading down her chest. Her short brown hair was sleeked back.

"I'm Ildeko," she said in a heavy European accent as she extended her hand.

She was stylish to a fault. Dripped money. Opinionated. Untouchable.

Among the many, one response in particular caught my attention. There was no picture attached, so I didn't have a visual clue, but her written word was concise, succinct and on point. I read it ten times. Her online

247

name was not just an ordinary Robin, but 'Rockin' Robin.' Her last name was Weede, and as she later would clarify to clerks taking telephone orders, Cablevision techies or little old ladies, "Weede, like in marijuana with an e at the end." A motion to her lips accompanied those words as if taking a pull on a fake cigarette. Most of the time people laughed, as they observed this silver haired woman mimic toking up.

We met after weeks of emails and phone calls. Our first date was in a traditional Japanese restaurant. I arrived a few minutes late. She was inside the restaurant, keeping an eye towards the large windows in the front. We easily made eye contact.

A quick tilt of her head said, "Come on in. It's me. I see you."

No words, just gestures. I smiled back and walked to her table. I liked her preppy look and we discussed our *Planet Out* profiles as women in traditional Japanese garb, bowed, delivered sushi rolls and tea and bowed again as they backed away. An old world of traditional gender-based values encountered two women on their first Internet date.

In person, Robin was more verbose and spoke excitedly about her work as a director of community education at a well-positioned local hospital and her role as an adjunct professor at Hofstra University. She was not a highbrow academic type but rather her teaching was grounded in real world experience in medicine and nursing science. She had two Masters' degrees and was published in several journals.

There was no doubt that she was raised on Long Island (Lawn-guy-land). Her accent gave her away. As I passionately love the English language, it was a challenge to hear the R's dropped on some words, like rememba instead of remember. Sista was used instead of sister. Yet she would throw an 'R' in at the end of the word idea, making it idear. All the Rs evened out in the end, adding one here and removing another there. I'd have to adjust and work my hardest not to lose any more of my Irish accent. Pronunciation is after all just a regional characteristic and not at all significant to the wonderful person I would come to know and love. Robin, I was beginning to see, was a 'what you see is what you get' kind of person. The first date ended with a handshake and a sense of relief that neither of us had two heads.

"I'll call you," I said as we parted, and I did the next night.

The following week we met again in the same place but by chance at a more intimate table. We removed our shoes and stepped into a private, low-seated booth area across from each other. Alone in a public place, but with the privacy of our own room. Awkward.

"This is nice and private," Robin said.

"Yeah." I smiled and wondered if she'd be the one.

Our waitress wore a colorful floral kimono and held two steaming hot towels to cleanse our hands as she opened the curtain.

"Oh, you both here last week? Welcome back," she said with a smile. "My name Sally," and took our orders for hot sake, miso soup, a bento box and assorted sushi rolls.

"I close curtain," she said.

She bowed and nodded as she ceremonially closed the curtains.

In between the spicy tuna roll and vegetable tempura, we got down to the really pressing questions.

Cats and dogs. She said "no cats" on her profile and I had two. "What made you ignore that?" she asked.

"Well, cats are such fabulous creatures. I'd hoped we could work that out if all else was good." She pondered my answer.

"I have two dogs, small ones, Chinese Crested. Have you ever heard of them?"

"Never," I said, thinking they must be some exotic breed.

She went on to explain the two types, a hairless and a powder-puff.

"The more hairless, the less teeth."

Charmingly odd but interesting, I thought. I was not a big dog person, but were these real dogs?

Travel distance was another difference in our profiles. It was the second area I thought could be adapted. She wanted to travel only six miles from her home to keep the dating in the neighborhood. I was about twenty-five miles away, certainly not in another state but not six miles.

"Wait. Do you want children or do you have any stashed away somewhere?" she asked.

"No children. Just extended family and me. Nieces and nephews," I said.

She valued nature. I loved Manhattan. There was room for growth.

Then she told me she was Jewish. My most fulfilling and fun relationships had been with independent and strong Jewish women. They grew up with knowledge of their history and a value system that grew out of it. We both felt alienated from mainstream traditional religious thinking for good reason.

It was our second date, not the first, so I accepted her invitation to go back to her house to meet the dogs. As we entered the living room, this beautiful small creature pranced out like a thoroughbred to investigate. The dog and I stopped short and stared at each other. Her ears stood straight up around the crest of flowing fine white hair cascading onto her face and down her back. Hair covered each ankle and a fluffy tail wagged back and forth. The rest of her was naked with skin that was smooth with characteristic spots. She was a sight to behold and demanded immediate respect. Her name was Versailles, after the Gardens of Versailles where Robin had recently visited. The degree of grooming needed, like the gardens, earned her the name. The second dog was a black powder puff with a white stripe down the center of her chest and a full coat of hair. Robin named her Haley after Alex Haley, the author of *Roots*. She was more reserved but also elegant.

It was clear to me that Robin was devoted to her dogs and they to her. She proudly displayed their small room with pictures plastered on the walls along with winning ribbons for first prize and best in show.

They were different. I liked them. She was different. I liked her. Our attraction was mutual but we both were good with delaying intimacy until we knew each other better. I took the twenty-five mile drive home feeling happy and looking forward to when I would see her again. I wished the distance between us were only six miles. Perhaps we would be our own best in life, our own best in show.

Chapter 18

I started wondering what it would be like to sleep with her, to hold her close to me. To be exposed once again. Dangling on the verge of vulnerability. The call of courage sounded. No pretense. No promises. No power.

I am an incurable and delighted deviant. I must forge my own path.

When I did sleep in her bed, it was not planned. After dinner at the Blue Adobe, a southwestern restaurant in her neighborhood, I got into my favorite off-white Buick Riviera. As she waved goodnight, I turned the ignition key, but my car would not start. A sly smile she was trying to suppress crossed her face.

"I guess you have to stay the night," she said as I rolled down the window.

"I . . . I guess I do. It's too late to call a mechanic."

She smiled.

The decision was taken out of our hands as I fell into her arms and into her bed. We didn't sleep much that night.

Meeting her parents weeks later was the next step. Robin's dad opened the front door the second we hit the driveway. She flew into his arms for a hug as I followed a few steps behind her. Then he did something I'll never forget. He reached one arm out to me to include me in their embrace. They were two of a kind.

Shirley approached smiling, looking sharp and bedazzled with bling from head to toe.

"Welcome. Come, sit," she said, gesturing us into the house.

Another shiksa! she's thinking.

Larry picked up Happy Hostess chicken for dinner. A family-owned caterer on Long Island, they provided the entire meal from matzo ball soup, to chicken prepared any way you want it, to fresh baked rugelach. Shirley made the cranberry and pineapple dressing. That was her specialty at all meals. Ordering in was the next best thing to making reservations in the Weede household.

Shirley plied me with questions.

"You work in a hospital?"

"How do you manage dealing with those crazy people you take care of?"

"Have a candy." She pushed the dish of wrapped chocolates towards me.

Larry spoke of their recent trip to Turkey and produced little souvenirs they bought.

Both parents spoke of their membership in Parents of Gays, an organization of support and activism.

"I think they've gone to more gay parades than I have," said Robin.

This Oceanside house was home for forty-six years after the small family of four migrated to the suburbs from Brooklyn, like many Jews of the time, seeking further assimilation and the good things in life. Robin was four and her sister six and a half. The small hamlet had been known as Christian Hook in colonial times, named for the religion of the settlers. It became Oceanville and then Oceanside as the bay and waterfront area became famous for seafood, especially oysters sold to New York City markets. The small ranch style house had a circular driveway and a lovely small garden in the back with an apple tree.

Robin's kindergarten teacher wrote on her report card, "Robin is vivacious and full of fun."

Vivacious comes from the Latin and means, "to live vigorously." The Weedes did and Robin did . . . Whether it was at the cabana rented each summer at Lido Beach, evenings at Nathans, which in the early years was an entertainment destination, or fishing and clamming in the local canals, they had a good time.

Robin was aware of being different at an early age. Whether it was being Jewish and living in a Christian neighborhood or that her interests were clearly those of a tomboy, she embraced who she was. The contrast was clear within her own home, as her sister and mother were definitely the girly, fashionable types.

"Honey, here's a pink dress Lena can't fit into anymore. It will look pretty on you. Go ahead and put it on so we can see you in it," her mother coaxed.

"I hate it. You know I hate pink," she said as she appeared from her bedroom, twisting the waist and pulling at the neck.

"I'm not wearing it. It's ugly. I want my own clothes, not hers."

"It's definitely not you," Lena said.

Her differentness sometimes led her to thoughtful, solitary play in the back garden in her favorite shorts, throwing a Spaulding ball onto the roof and catching it with her right and left hands for hours as it bounced in either direction.

It was in the garden space that Robin began to find her place in the world, in the universe. There were warm days and nights when she would lie on the grass and stare at the sky, comfortable with feeling separate from everything but at the same time an important part of something much greater.

She wondered what the stars and moon were made of that lit the sky above her home. The sounds of the night delighted her whether it was the crickets singing in unison or a sea bird winging its way home. She thought about her life and how she would fit into this bewildering and amazing world. She was at peace exploring the sky and thinking there was nothing she couldn't do. Larry sometimes joined her on the grass and they talked about nature and life in general.

"You see those bumble bees jumping from flower to flower?" Larry asked her. "They are carrying the pollen that makes other plants grow. Everything out here in the garden depends on everything else to survive. They never stop, those bees. Very hard working and loyal to the queen bee," he added.

"So, they're good to have around, even though they can sting you," Robin replied.

"Yep. It's their garden too. We have to respect them."

Important questions were asked and answered.

259

Why do lightening bugs light up? Is it okay to hold that worm in my hand?

Can we catch that frog? Am I a tomboy? This awareness of nature, of uniqueness and union, would forever guide her journey.

Her dad loved nature and each summer grew a garden of vegetables, scientifically fertilized by elephant poop taken from the local circus grounds and transported in the boot of the car. Much to the chagrin of Shirley and Lena, the lingering aroma filled their nostrils on their weekend car outings to visit the beloved grandparents in Brooklyn. Robin likes the smell of elephant poop to this day.

The satisfaction of caring for others was awakened during these visits to her grandmother. Anna had severe diabetes.

"Can I give you the insulin shot?" she pleaded in her teenage years.

The glass syringe with stainless steel needle was carefully placed in her hands. She drew the insulin into the syringe and with the expertise of a well-practiced nurse, administered the shot. It was the highlight of her week.

"I'm going to become a nurse," she announced on the ride home one day.

"Uugh. You'll be dealing with blood and guts," Lena responded.

"What about helping people get better, or stopping someone's pain?" Robin said.

"Nursing is a great profession. We'll always need nurses," Larry said.

Her mother agreed. "Solid salary too. You won't have to worry about a job."

Through the darkness shone a very welcome light as the heavy curtains of the past rose, and Rockin' Robin and Maeve began their own female pas de deux. In ballet, a pas de deux is a type of duet. It usually consists of an entrée, adagio, two variations (one for each dancer), and a coda. The adagio is slow and elaborate partnering, demonstrating each dancer's strength and grace, providing support and paired movements. It includes holding, lifting and balancing that would be impossible to do on one's own. The variations are when each of the two performs independently to demonstrate her unique abilities and skills. The coda is the conclusion, incorporating all elements and allows a looking back to view a simplified whole.

For us the choreography was familiar. We were conscious of the gift of looking back and choosing with awareness in the present. On this new stage perfection was not the goal. It was a call late in life to truly grow up. It was neither codependency nor a prescription to live by shoulds and oughts, nor worries about what others thought. It was an investment to move forward in a journey together. We were not falling head over heels in love, but we were falling into a loving relationship with our eyes wide open.

Robin owned a ranch house and rented her basement apartment to a friend, Chris, who was a very important figure in the lesbian bar scene on Long Island. Chris created a space where young and older women could come and socialize and safely spend the evening.

Reminiscing about her working days, she said, "I felt like a freedom rider in the civil rights movement. A lot of people didn't want us in the neighborhood, but we held our ground. We formed a community that was safe and fun."

Talking to Robin and me as we sat at her bar enjoying a Corona and lime, Chris said, "I hope you are not going to fulfill the old lesbian joke about renting a U-Haul on the second date."

"Oh no," we both replied. "This relationship will develop in slow motion."

I rented the top floor of my house to make ends meet. We took turns staying over in each other's place, meeting friends, visiting family, traveling, and strengthening our bonds of love and friendship.

After four years of dating, Robin moved into my house and rented hers. It seemed life had turned around for both of us. But living together? This was the real test.

Chapter 19

I never understood the destruction and competition within human families until I visited the Galapagos Islands and met the blue-footed boobies.

Robin and I disembarked from our boat, the La Pinta, for a dry landing on North Seymour Island in the Galapagos Islands. June was a perfect time to tour with two of our best friends, Ann and Marni, along with eight other travellers. Carlos, a native of Ecuador continued our education for the day about a natural world of protected birds, iguanas, penguins, and tortoises that lived on different islands, unafraid of people.

"Okay, my friends. Remember, we stay on the path and together. We're guests on their land. No feeding or approaching any of the birds we are about to see. We're not to disturb them."

Carlos oozed a passion for these islands. His English blended with native Spanish that made him a perfect naturalist guide for the Galapagos.

"Here you will have your first encounter with blue-footed boobies. The seabirds are called boobies because of their ungainly bright blue feet that flop when walking on land. The bluer the feet, the more fertile the bird. In the air and when they dive for food, they are majestic. In their nesting homes, they are lethal. Let's meet some further down the path."

Blue-footed boobies lined either side of the path. Their webbed feet looked like big blue duck feet beneath a massive body with a wingspan of five feet. A male lifted his bright blue feet in the air demonstrating his virility. Birds faced each other and lifted their beaks, pointing to the sky as far as they could reach. Each movement determined the ultimate outcome of the dance.

"See the other female on the side? She's waiting to see how this finishes. She's interested in him," Carlos whispered to us.

We stood for ten minutes enthralled by the birds at our feet, unabashed and unconcerned about our presence. Time demanded we move on. On the next stretch we watched the blue-footed boobies plunge as a group into the sea for food. A booby sat on two eggs further down the rookery, a testimony to the results of another courtship.

Carlos stopped and asked, "How many of you have brothers and sisters?"

Ten of us raised our hands.

"How many of you can relate to sibling rivalry?"

I raised my hand along with the other nine.

"The second bird to hatch will be pecked to death by the first. Competition for food is fierce. The parents look on and do nothing. In fact, parents are known to attack small boobies from other nests if they have the chance."

I asked, remembering my own sibling rivalry, "Carlos, are you saying humans act the same way?"

He responded with a smile, "Yeah, to a certain degree. Human siblings may not be very kind to each other when it comes to parental attention and their share of the goods."

"I like to think of what happens here as Greek tragedy in the Galapagos," replied Carlos. "Look, there is an adult going after a newborn to the right. Oh God, I can't believe we're seeing this. Got too far away from his mother. Wait. Wait. The mother is coming over. Probably her only surviving offspring this time. Watch. Watch." A head on battle ensued and the baby bird flopped away to its nest site. The mother triumphed.

I fell down a memory hole. Lost with images from the past.

Mom's telephone call when she first told me she had colon cancer first came to mind.

"I'm riddled with it," she said.

Pictures and thoughts of Mom's funeral that had been carefully wrapped and locked away, popped open. Scenes of angst and lasting hurt. Recognizable, despite their age.

The uneven ground jarred my body as my mind descended against my will and brought the past into the present. The rest of the island was a blur that afternoon. The sea breeze calmed me.

"Maeve, are you okay?" Robin asked. "What's wrong?"

"I'll tell you when we get back on the ship."

The small ship dining room, dotted with portholes that framed the islands in the distance, was set for dinner. We sank into the royal blue armchairs exhausted from our island walking. Every corner of the room burst with the home cooked aroma of arroz con pollos. My thoughts settled on ideas of home and the blue-footed boobies. Ann intuited the impact of booby family relationships and asked, "I loved looking at the boobies, but can you believe how brutal they are?"

"I grew up with a sister who was totally opposite to me," Robin said. "We were very different and my mother, without even knowing she was doing it, encouraged our competition to get her approval. I took after my Dad who was outgoing and just loved people. I didn't need to be in the middle of that."

Marni agreed that sayings like *Blood is thicker than water,* family loyalty, and family secrets were sacred in her upbringing. "But now I stay away from my brothers to keep my sanity."

The waiter, attentive to the intensity of our conversation, arrived with another bottle.

"Ladies, may I?"

"Definitely. Oh yes," we said in unison.

The Chilean wine fueled the therapy discussion. It swirled in the glasses as the ship gently swayed its way forward to the next island.

"We presented a happy face to the outside world, but beneath the surface were many fractures that broke wide open as we got older," Ann shared as she took another large sip.

"Well the blue footed boobies and my family have a lot in common," I said.

"Tell them what happened at your Mom's funeral," Robin said.

'Well, we didn't have actual murder stains, but we could have.

Gerard, Grainne and I were thrust into a surreal drama, cast in our childhood roles. We reenacted ancient conflicts. The three of us were dressed as adults. We each drove cars. We each had successful careers, bank accounts and families. But feelings that accumulated through the years took over.

I grew up with a sense of family unity lasting forever. That illusion shattered when Mom died. Mom wanted us to all get along. Peace at all cost. She was the glue. When she died we became unglued."

Grainne and I drove to Baxter as fast as we could when we got the call from Gerard.

"Come now and don't stop on the way."

She was awake in bed when we got there. Her eyes lit up as she reached for us to come closer. We hugged her.

Her familiar taupe leather bag lay open on her bed. Inside was the story of her life. Her wallet held a yellowed picture of Dad, pictures of Grainne and Michael and each of her grandchildren, Gerard in a group picture of his family, small shots of his first two daughters in black and white, a picture of me with both of them in Catskill, her Social Security and Medicare cards, a holy card in remembrance of her mother and brother and a lock of Thomas' baby hair. A small well-used pamphlet to pray the Novena to Our Lady of Knock was in a side pocket.

Strong. Full of wisdom. Always there. Now her frail body lay on her bed, her fervent spirit departing. Her eyes communicated her love and final concern. She tried to have her personal things in order and in a weakened voice, once again explained the plans she made.

"I have labeled items with your names on masking tape. Some are gifts you bought in your travels or things you made." She nodded toward the stained glass jewelry box I made that sat on her bureau. "Maeve, take that with you."

"Take the box out from underneath the bed," she asked one afternoon when she had a little more strength, in between medications.

"It has my jewelry in it. I made three bags, one for each of you." She pointed with her bruised hand for us to open it. We looked at what she had arranged. Dad's ring was in mine.

"Gerard has a letter I want you to read when the three of you are together after I die." She reached her hands out to ours as we sat close together on the bed.

I wanted to cry, but held it in.

She knew.

"I want the three of you to get along, to be there for each other."

She fell asleep.

The next morning a soft June air crept into her small bedroom through the slightly open window. It gently blew the fine lace curtains. It was noiseless in the street seven stories below. A small vase of red roses that arrived in the mail a few days before perfumed the darkness from her dresser. Grainne and I knew her heart would stop any moment. We sat silently, she on Mom's ottoman and I on the bottom edge of her double bed as we witnessed her breathing peacefully subside. Statues of The Infant of Prague and the Sacred Heart stood by and carried her final prayers to heaven.

A solemn stillness filled the room.

I was numb. Speechless. We looked at each other, acknowledging our pain and terrible loss.

"I'm glad we were here with her," Grainne said.

"Yes."

She called Gerard at work.

Within minutes Mom's skin seemed to fade and lose all remaining color. Gerard came within twenty minutes and without a word, knelt alone at the end of her bed, grasped the rosary beads from her bedside table and laid it on her body. He began saying the Hail Mary and the Our Father. Grainne and I stared at him in disbelief as we stood on the far side of the bed.

"What is he doing? This is so out of character for him. He is an atheist. We are both here," she whispered to me.

Stephen Dedalus, the literary hero of *Ulysses* was tormented for the remainder of his lifetime because he refused to kneel at his mother's deathbed to pray. Months later, I thought Gerard must have had this image in mind when he knelt without saying a word. He, like us, had just lost his greatest supporter.

As the funeral employees came through the door to remove Mom's body, Gerard announced, "I want to call a meeting this evening to discuss the funeral arrangements."

"A meeting?" Grainne responded. "Are you kidding? You are not at work."

He went to the living room and retrieved the sealed letter Mom had left with instructions on the envelope for us to "open together" after she died.

"Let's open the letter now. We're together. It's what Mom wanted," I said.

"I don't want it opened until after she is buried."

"We have a right to hear our mother's words, especially in this moment," I replied with outrage. "Why not?"

"I am the administrator of her estate. No."

He hurriedly left the apartment without another word, securing her letter and her rosary beads in his breast pocket.

At the scheduled evening meeting, we decided on coffin bearers and that Robin would be one. Other details were decided like the meeting time with the funeral parlor and readers for the service.

The next morning Gerard arrived and announced, "I've changed my mind. Robin can't be a coffin bearer because it would create an imbalance and is not traditional. I have other friends I'm going to include."

"An imbalance? She can carry a coffin along with the other people. That's ridiculous. We agreed last night," I said.

Gerard pulled up his posture and bolted toward the apartment door. He threw his head backwards as he left.

"You are trying to further your gay agenda. I won't do it," he shouted.

"What?"

I fell into the couch. Held my head to steady my thoughts, to control my mounting anger and despair.

"There is no gay agenda. I just want Robin to have a real role in the service. Who does he think he is?"

"I know," said Grainne.

I knew at this point reason had gone out the door with him. I knew he would never treat me as an equal.

Gerard gave us the time for the funeral parlor meeting one hour later than scheduled. We called to check beforehand and were present at the table when he arrived. He stopped short when he saw us, but couldn't say; "I told you an hour later."

He attempted to exclude Grainne and me.

Amigone (Am I Gone) was ironically the name of the funeral parlor, pounding home the harsh reality, that she truly was gone. We were gone; family as we knew it was gone.

The family business included a gay relative assigned to Mom's burial arrangements.

"I'm gay. I'm so sorry for what is going on. Gerard is a piece of work," he said in hushed tones as he pulled me to the side. "I'll take care of things."

Grainne wanted a female bag piper to play at Mom's coffin as we entered the church. She located one. Gerard asked for her name and number, pretending it was for a written program. Grainne replied, "Why do you need her telephone number for the program?"

He was going to cancel her.

The day of the service, tensions were sky high. Some of Gerard's friends and colleagues offered condolences when they spoke to Grainne and me.

"Oh, I didn't know Gerard had sisters. He never mentioned you."

The bagpiper played outside the church. Gerard and his wife were not in place to lead the procession into the church behind the coffin. Robin and I were.

"Let's go!" Robin said as she quickly identified the confusion. We led the walk up the aisle directly behind Mom's coffin. The organ music pulsated as my heart pounded in my chest. Lub-dub--lub-dub--lub-dub . . .

The choir sang *Libera me, Domine* .

Free me, lord from death eternal

On that day of dread...

That day, day of anger, of calamity and misery,

That day, the day of great and exceeding bitterness.

A walk of triumph filled with loss. Filled with anguish, tears and tribulation.

Gerard gave the eulogy.

"I loved my mother," he began.

Grainne and I were mentioned once as accompanying Mom to America.

A short gathering took place at Gerard's home following the service. He pulled us into a corner to read Mom's letter. The one paged scripted words had directions for the trip to Catskill and a plea for us to take care of each other.

"You've read the letter. Nothing that we didn't know," he said.

I placed it in my pocket to keep.

The room filled with neighbors and work companions.

"I'm so sorry for your loss. Gerard never learned to not be the center of attention," an old colleague of his whispered in my ear.

Grainne had two cars between her and her children. I was driving down to Catskill with them where Mom would be buried beside Dad. We gathered the things she wanted us to have, most labeled with our names, and small pieces of furniture for Grainne. Memories of our growing up. Memories of her. Grainne told Gerard ahead of time.

The final blows to our family as we knew it were dealt in the fury and blindness of our grief when we arrived in Catskill.

"You stole Mom's things from her apartment. I want them returned. I want a list right away. I will distribute her things," Gerard yelled into the phone..

"There will be no list. Those are items Mom wanted us to have. We are her daughters," Grainne said in return.

"I'm calling the police," he said.

Fear and disbelief paralyzed us. I lost it. Crying. Outraged. Crying again.

"Is this really happening? This is Mom's funeral." I knew Mom's reactions and this would have shattered her.

Her words, "get along, support each other," hopelessly forgotten.

We buried her, but not in peace. We didn't stand beside our older brother. We couldn't. Childhood rivalries frozen in time melted at our feet. The fragile bonds of family unity lay beside Mom's lifeless body.

Chapter 20

My practice of Catholicism consistently lessened since I left the convent. Nothing changed in the church since my departure. I heard the same old talk . . . dusty dead buzzwords that had no relevance.

The Catholic religion had worked for Mom. It kept her grounded and gave her hope.

In the years after her death, I remembered her devotion. I pictured the earnestness of her praying, the sincerity of her belief. It just didn't work for me. I remembered the failure of the priest to acknowledge my sister and me at Mom's funeral. Many times I seethed inside as I listened to the fiery sermons of other inept and hypocritical priests.

"Look at the lilies of the field, and see how God takes care of them."

So you don't have to do anything or worry about anything as long as you believe?

"I have been crucified with Christ. It is no longer I who live, but Christ who lives in me."

It's not about my family or me. Suppress those individual thoughts and urges.

When I sat beside Mom at Mass, meaningless words agitated me. I wanted to stand up and shout out a challenging question to the all-knowing priest and the subservient congregation.

So, are you saying we don't have to think, act, and question?

Everything will be ok as long as we have faith? How do your words transfer to the real world, to real people?

Mom knelt beside me, head bowed deep in meditation… with the rest of the congregation. Occasionally I caught her eyeing me. She liked that I attended Mass with her. I did it for her and kept my mouth shut. I imagined she prayed earnestly for all her family. Her eyes met mine during the handshake of "Peace be with you." Her expression said it all.

I'm glad you're here, even though you don't really want to be.

We talked on the walk home from Church.

"I have a hard time with what the priest said today about women and marriage. What do you think about what they are saying?"

"What do I think?" She paused. "I think there's a lot of old men with old ideas. I go to pray and receive communion. I think women should be allowed to become priests and priests be able to marry."

"Wow. I'm impressed. That's pretty revolutionary thinking about the church. I do miss religion in my life. The dogma just kills it for me. I like to go with you, though."

Mom wasn't one to fight a lost battle with her children. She hoped her quiet influence and prayers would work.

"I just worry about you, that's all," she said.

281

"I know."

I learned to live without the god I once loved. I felt
homesick but not able to return to the home of the
religion I knew. Years passed. I persisted in wanting a
place to express my spirituality.

Carl Jung so perfectly expressed the essential
dilemma.

"The question is not religion or not, but which kind
of religion, whether it is one furthering development, the
unfolding of specifically human powers, or one
paralyzing them . . ."

I went religion shopping. A hundred-year-old, plain
wooden building stood in the middle of a busy shopping
area in the town where I lived. It was a Quaker House. A
friend and I opened the doors to a half filled room of
people sitting in silence. Silence was something I had
experience with. The wooden pews were as basic as they
could get. There were no words on the wall, no pulpit,
no handout for the morning program. I didn't know what
to expect.

When are the directions going to come? Will someone do a reading? No hymns either? No priest. I knew no priest. So, no sermons either? Good.

You show up and wait to "hear the voice of God within." Quaker services, I learned, were entirely self-directed, leaderless.

It was a little like the play *Waiting for Godot.* In that play nothing happened and yet the audience was glued to their seats.

The little voice within said, "Get the hell out of here, before you lose it completely."

Too much was missing in terms of the obvious trappings of religion.

The Unitarian church offered great promise, especially with its long history of supporting gay and lesbian issues. The French Gothic architecture surprised me. The Church was a former Long Island farmhouse and setting for Renaissance Fairs before purchased. Colorful banners represented the beliefs and universal values of the Unitarian movement. A single flame in stained glass overlooked the congregation room. It was a lively environment. The people I met were liberal minded, involved with political issues and I felt welcomed. Everyone was welcomed. A lay leader for the morning service introduced herself as a "recovering Catholic."

"Me too," I said.

I attended many times but in the end, found it spiritually wanting.

This isn't really working for me.

I stopped religion shopping.

A number of years later on a perfectly sunny day in October, I woke up and left a message on my boss' phone.

"Sorry, Steve, but I'm not feeling well. I'm taking a personal day. Nothing pressing on my schedule. Call if you need me."

Ah, so good, a mental health day. I have the entire day to myself and I am feeling perfectly fine.

I looked at a book on my nightstand that I had finished the night before. The *Red Tent* by Anita Diamant.

I'll start the day at my favorite bookstore in town to pick up her new novel.

The Book Revue opened at 10 a.m. I waited outside reading the notices of visiting authors. Plastered dead center on the window was a picture of Anita Diamant, announcing a book signing for her new book, *Good Harbor.*

Are you kidding? That's weird. The exact book I want. Shit. It's not till tonight.

The first one in the door, I went straight for the display table of the visiting author. I stood reading the first few pages.

This is not grabbing me like her first book. I hate the beginning. Not getting it.

I placed it back on the table. Beside it was a book titled, *Choosing a Jewish Life*. It was not the kind of book I had in mind that morning, but I was intrigued.

What does this mean, Choosing a Jewish Life? Aren't you either Christian or Jewish?

I never thought of being able to move from one to the other, to cross over.

Sid often teased me.

"Maeve, you're a wanna-be-Jew."

I sat on the wood plank floor of the old store, leaned against the stonewall, and began to read. The store cat named Marmelade brushed up beside me. She often got petted by the customers and meowed in my face as she reached a paw for the book. As I ran my hand down her soft fur, I saw the words, "Jew by Choice," and sat straight up. Marmalade ran off for a more available customer.

With the book on the seat beside me, I drove home to devour its contents. Such discovery must be accompanied with a cool glass of chardonnay regardless of the early time of day. I curled up on the couch with cheese and crackers and chardonnay and my new book.

It spoke to something dearly missed in my life. Reform Judaism, the most liberal of Jewish traditions was committed to inclusion and adapting to a changing culture. The absence of dogma was striking.

Now there's a novel approach for a religion.

I heard the key turn in the front door. Robin was home. She came into the family room with her usual excitement, glad to be home and out of the hospital for another day.

"How was your day?" I asked.

"Crazy as usual," she answered. "I hate people who have slept their way to the top. They don't know what they're doing."

It was a conversation we often had.

"I have something to tell you," I said. "I found a book today that sort of blew my mind. It's about converting to Judaism."

She sat down, looked at me and said nothing. I handed her the book.

"Well . . . I . . . really . . . *Choosing a Jewish Life*. Are you serious?"

"It strikes such a strong chord in me. I haven't been able to put the book down. I am serious. I went to Book Revue for Anita Diamont's new novel and this was next to it."

Robin was at a serious loss for words. She fell back on the couch, staring at the book, then at me. We talked for a long time after she recovered.

"I'm Jewish. I just haven't been in a synagogue since I was a kid. I don't think it was an accident that you found this book. How about if we do it together?" she said. "I would love to study Reform Judaism with you."

"Wow. I can't believe you're saying that. We have to find a Reform Temple around here."

As I stepped into the shower the following morning, I shivered at the thoughts swirling through my mind.

How can I renounce the religion of my family, of my birth?

Am I betraying my ancestors in Ireland? Surely they would turn over in their graves at the thought.

Voices from the graveyards spoke. Personalities of the past asserted their disapproval.

How can you turn your back on your religion and you having been a nun?

Heretic. I want nothing to do with you anymore.

I became scared once again to step out on my own. Scared of being rejected. Afraid that people I loved today couldn't overcome the shock. Would they think I was rejecting them? It wouldn't matter if they weren't practicing Catholicism anymore. They could go back at any time. I would be out, converted, something different.

I called my good friend Sid. "I'm thinking about converting to Reform Judaism."

Her first response was to laugh. Then she got a hold of herself.

"Maeve, why now? What's going on?"

"I feel there's been a hole in my life, something missing."

"OK. But any organized religion comes with a lot of outdated rules. Maybe Reform is different. I hope this isn't because I taught you Yiddish."

"It doesn't sound like Reform Judaism is, from what I've read," I said. "Maybe I'm meshugah. I think my family might freak."

"Maeve, we've talked about this stuff before. Knowing you as a very spiritual person, you need to do what is right for you. Don't worry what other people think. That's their issue. What does Robin think?"

"She's excited, engaged and wants to learn her religion with me."

"You know I can't say I'm surprised, knowing you. That both of you want to do it together is great. You'll be able to teach me a few things. I bet the family won't even care. It's not like they're going to church themselves."

"As usual, you cut to the heart of the matter," I said.

The next Saturday was Gay Pride Day near our home in Huntington. Robin and I liked to go to walk through the crowds, visit the booths and hear the music. It was always so energizing to be present. We felt the pride. It was packed. Rainbow flags were everywhere. Long Island businesses were represented like banks, travel agencies, hospitals, dog and cat rescues, and local food vendors. We slowly made our way through the crowd, wearing our well-worn gay pride t-shirts. In the middle of everything was a booth titled, Temple Beth El of Huntington. I gingerly approached, not knowing what to say or ask.

"Hi. I'm Judy, a member of Temple Beth El." A good-looking woman in her 40s quickly extended her hand as she flashed a warm smile.

"Temple Beth El is a Reform Temple a few blocks away. Are you Jewish?"

"I am but haven't been practicing," replied Robin.

"I am not but I want to learn about Reform Judaism. I'm thinking of converting."

"Debby will be back in a while. She's a convert and would love to talk to you. I can tell you TBE is a wonderful place."

Judy spoke about the female cantor and the rabbi, "who are the best," and invited us to attend Friday night services the following week.

And so we entered the doors of Temple Beth El in Huntington, New York the next week and everything changed. I felt like a stranger in a strange land, but not for long. Judy spotted us and immediately came over to welcome us.

"I'm so glad you decided to come. You'll love it here," she said.

The interior lacked the pomp and circumstance of Catholic Churches. No statues adorned the walls as Judaism does not use religious icons as symbols. Large wood beams resembling an arc, like Noah's Ark, supported the ceiling and large modern, colorful stained glass windows overlooked the bema. Simple and sacred at the same time. A choir of red headed, blond and brown haired children sang the opening song, accompanied by the rabbi on the guitar. They could have been from anywhere in the world. My image of a rabbi with a long hairy beard quickly vanished. The words used in the service were gender neutral. Robin and I were moved by the richness of the language and thoughtful open discussion about contemporary issues as Jeffrey the rabbi posed a question to the community. An elderly long time member named Sylvia, turned around from the seat in front of us to say, "I have not seen you here before. Welcome to Temple Beth El."

On the way home, as we both were taking it all in, Robin said, "Wow. I think this was meant to be."

We enrolled in a six-month Introduction to Judaism course in a Temple an hour away from home with six other interfaith couples. I remained skeptical, waiting for the part that didn't make sense, the hidden organized religion turn-off, the "you must believe this or that" but it didn't happen. Our teacher, a short and plump convert herself, had a passion for teaching and imparting the basics of Reform Judaism.

We began each class by singing together Hine Ma Tove.

"How good it is, and how pleasant to dwell together in unity."

Translated, these were the same words sung in Latin at the end of the Novitiate ceremony when I became a bride of Christ. It was called Ecce Quam Bonum from Psalm 133 of the Book of Psalms.

We discussed some of the basic thinking in Reform Judaism like "Tikkun Olam" which literally means "world repair." It is commonly used to refer to the pursuit of social action and social justice. The description of holiness or "Kedushah" or rendering each day with the intention to do good, to live righteously.

"Mitzvot" derived from the Torah is the way to put words into action through compassion and kindness in daily life. These traditions resonated with my first held beliefs.

I took it the next step and asked our young, smart and sensitive rabbi to be my sponsor for conversion.

"You know your situation is one of the more unusual ones, having been in religious life and choosing to convert," he said.

"Yes. It makes it all the more powerful for me, the more meaningful."

He suggested books for me to read. We talked. He asked me the traditional question three times.

"Are you sure you want to convert?"

On each occasion, I said, "Yes" and we discussed the ramifications.

We picked a date for my conversion after months of meeting and talking. It was Simchas Torah. This day is one of my favorite holidays as the entire Torah is rolled out from beginning to end. The last portion for the year is first read and then the beginning, to start the entire cycle of reading anew.

There is no literal interpretation of the Torah in Reform Judaism. It is read, interpreted and applied to what is real for you and happening in today's world. It is a very sacred object and on this holiday, it is passed around to anyone who wants to hold it and dance with it. I'll never forget the rabbi handing it over to me, as I held it against my chest like you would a newborn, and danced about in circles with the community. Transporting. Exhilarating.

It seems all religions have water as a symbol of renewal and rebirth. The mikvah is part of the rite of conversion to Judaism. An actual mikvah bath exists and I immersed my body in the water as the mikvah attendant and Robin looked on.

After three full immersions, I then recited aloud in Hebrew the *shehehiyanu,* a blessing of thanksgiving said at special moments in life.

Baruch ata Adonai Eloheynu melech ha-olam, shehehiyanu, vekiamanu, vehigianu lazman hazeh.

"Blessed are you, ruler of the universe who have kept us alive, sustained us and enabled us to reach this moment."

At that point I heard the cantor and rabbi break into song outside the door. I felt spiritually high and good about my decision to convert. I was primordially happy.

The Beit Din or Rabbinic Court was next where I met with the cantor, the rabbi and another rabbi from a nearby temple. It wasn't a test about my knowledge of Reform Judaism, though I felt I was going for an oral examination on just that. The meeting was a discussion and re-affirmation of my intention to convert.

"Maeve, there's no need to be nervous. You'll be fine." Jeffrey warmly assured me before going into his office for the meeting. "It's really a formality." His words helped but I was a nervous wreck. I was sweating up a storm. It was so intimate, just the four of us.

"Tell us how you've come to the point of sitting with us here today?" Jeffrey started.

"It's been a long process. I can't identify with Catholicism any more. Not for years. I've missed religion in my life but need a place that will accept

Robin and me as a couple. I need a place that is actively involved with issues in the world. I studied Reform Judaism and identify with its philosophy."

"Have you started to practice having a Jewish home?" asked the cantor.

"Robin and I light the candles on Shabbat at home. We come to services often but we're really in the learning mode still."

"Learning is key to Reform Judaism, personally and as a community," said the visiting rabbi.

"How would you feel about not celebrating Christmas and the holidays you grew up with?" he asked.

I replied, "It will feel weird and I will miss what I had been used to for so long. It's more about family coming together and we will still do that."

The cantor asked, "Are you ready to identify as being a Jew? We do have a history of being singled out for persecution."

I responded, "I am already in a minority category as a gay woman. I'm used to it and yes I am."

Finally the evening for my conversion service came along and I would receive my Jewish name and speak to the congregation about my decision to convert. The synagogue was packed. Two containers of white lilies and vibrant greens adorned the bema for the holiday. The adult choir was in full and harmonious voice. Robin and I were so excited and happy. Sid and Steve, my other Jewish family, came to the service as witnesses.

I began my speech on the bema in an accentuated Irish accent.

"I suppose you might be wondering what a nice Irish Catholic girl like me is doing deciding to become a nice Jewish girl!" I got smiles and laughter and I continued my story. I told them it was a gift to be able to choose the religion that spoke to me as an adult and not merely follow what I believed in as a child. In these re-defining moments of choosing Reform Judaism, I honored my parents' memory in choosing my Jewish name, Uza Ana Yakova. Uza means strength in Hebrew and is also the meaning of my mother's name Bridget. Yakova is the Hebrew for Jacob, of which James, my father's name, is the English derivative. Ana was for Robin in memory of her grandmother. So there I was, from Maeve to Uza, from Catholic to Jew-by-choice.

Chapter 21

I'm the marrying kind. Becoming a bride of Christ with twenty-two other young and eager brides, was quite bizarre. I became a new kind of bride, a Rockin' Robin in the flesh and blood, kind of bride. A bride not yet recognized by the country I live in. United States Federal Law did not recognize marriage between same sex couples in 2008 and New York State didn't pass a non-discrimination law until 2011.

One of the shrinks sat down beside me in the cafeteria at lunchtime the week before Robin and I were heading to California to be married. He and Robin hit it off at a recent retirement party. She forced him to dance and he loved it. John never seemed to be happy. He was the brooding type, over-weight and a bit unkempt, usually sitting alone, spoke infrequently at medical staff meetings but spent lots of time with his patients. They loved him.

"Hey, John, Robin and I are going to tie the knot next week in California."

He hesitated a moment and then announced, "I don't believe in gay marriage. I mean, maybe two women, but I can't see two men raising a baby. Marriage ties you down, anyway."

Clearly he had his own issues.

"Well, I believe people have a right to affirm their love for each other through marriage, whether they are gay or straight."

He shrugged and started slurping on his Diet Coke as though it was the last he would ever have, unaware that his conversation had offended me. If he did know I was offended, I thought at the time he didn't care, as so many people feel it's okay to openly disapprove gay marriage and gay families, right to your face. I knew better than to pursue the conversation. It was not the time or place to try to open his heart and his mind. A few years later a friend told me he ran into him at a gay bar in New York City. He asked for me. He was scared about my openness and his own sexuality at that lunchtime conversation. I didn't know.

On the complete opposite end of the acceptance spectrum, Temple Beth El at the Friday night Shabbat before our trip, held a special celebration and blessing. The cantor arrived dressed in rainbow colors and blessed our union. We lit the Shabbat candles, separating the week from the beginning of Shabbat reflection and peace. The many who attended raised us on the chairs in the air and danced around us singing "Hava nagila. Hava nagila. Hava nagila ve-nismeha." It means, "Let's rejoice. Let's rejoice. Let's rejoice and be happy."

We both were filled with joy and gratitude that we found a place where people were educated and embracing or willing to learn. Love is love.

In May the California Supreme Court overturned the state's ban on same sex marriage, and 18,000 couples married. Robin and I will never forget completing the marriage license request at the county clerk's office in Long Beach. The paper-work had been completed online and we appeared in person at the window, nervous as all hell. The clerk was an elderly plump woman who had most likely asked the same questions her entire life: just not to same-sex couples. She held an exquisite power to perform her brief clerical duty with understanding and respect or personal scorn. She asked us standard questions with a jaded but official air, checked a few boxes and applied the seal of the county to the marriage application. At that moment I imagine she registered a change in her routine, a twist in her duties as she looked up into the faces of two women. The tediousness of her job was interrupted for a flash as she adjusted her gem studded glasses to sharpen her view.

"Congratulations," she said with a little smile.

"Thank you." We glowed back.

I cried. We both did.

It came from nowhere. It came from everywhere.

Together we walked out of the building, wrapped in each other's love and arms.

Robin and I were married under a rainbow chuppah by a female rabbi from Los Angeles in Long Beach Harbor. The sun was shining as we spoke our marriage vows. The rabbi signed our beautiful ketubah, or marriage contract with Steven and Sid as witnesses.

The ketubah reads, *We shall support each other in achieving spiritual, intellectual, and emotional fulfillment. We promise to be full and equal partners in life and to do everything in our power to permit each of us to become the persons we are yet to be. From this day forward, we are as one.*

Steven and his partner of a few years, Jim, were married with us on the same day on the same boat. We all had a quiet celebration with Sid, her partner and a few California friends. Our napkins said it all: 'Happily Hitched.' Today we probably would have thrown a big party in New York but a quiet elopement seemed the best choice at the time.

The next phase of life was calling loudly, bellowing in our ears. Retirement. Robin was the first to respond. She retired after forty-two years of working in the same organization. Simply put, she was 'burnt out' and tired of the politics. She had the "three-legged financial stool" in place: Social Security benefits, pension, and personal savings. Plus, she added a fourth leg, real estate. That made the stool very steady. She made it clear at her retirement party at the hospital that she was not joining the ranks of 'The Volunteers'. It was almost a given that anyone who stayed as long as she did could not pull themselves away from the daily hospital routine. She was going to reinvent herself, relax and do whatever she wanted. It wasn't all that easy at first. Casually she would say to me, "I'm going to stop in the office today," as though she was still employed and could just show up at any time. She'd find a way to drop something off or pick something up or just stop in to say hello. It was her way of transitioning from her work world of many years.

There is no way to predict the impact retirement will have on your life. I am by nature, a planner, a doer, a learner, a get-things-done kind of gal. My identity was not solely fixed on my career but the stress of leaving that identity behind landed me in a medical hospital after passing out at Home Depot. I laid down on the sheetrock and momentarily lost consciousness. Good planning for an unexpected collapse. Before I knew what was happening I was on a stretcher in an ambulance, glaring into the faces of what appeared to be two adolescent boys, posing as EMTs. One had a face full of untreated acne.

So this is how it ends?

"Well, you have just bought yourself a million-dollar workup," my medical doctor announced when he met me at the emergency room.

Three days later and just in time for my course on World Literature in the local college, I was discharged. "Etiology unknown" was the recurrent impression and conclusion on a CT of my brain, a cardiac workup and whatever else was checked. I did have a brain and I did have a heart and that was all I needed for entry into retirement and the next phase of life. A cruise to my favorite city, Venice and the Greek Islands with Steve and Jim marked the beginning of our new adventure.

A bit too young for full retirement, Medicare and Social Security, I landed a job within what was known as 'The System.' It was a true win/win situation until the age of 65. All the knowledge and insight I had about accreditation of psychiatric facilities, they needed. One of the highlights was being asked to survey North Pines with other surveyors before a purchase commitment was finalized. I knew where the bodies were buried. My old CEO, Steve looked at me across the boardroom table with his familiar broad smile and said,

"We'll just have to use all the things you taught us about distracting surveyors and getting through a survey successfully."

They did. I loved it. During those last years of belonging to the workforce, I contemplated retirement and how I would approach it. Many of my colleagues looked at me with amazement, opposing the idea and insisting that surely I was going to do consulting or teach at a local college. Neither inspired me. In certain ways I had been preparing for retirement my whole life.

"Aren't you afraid of being bored?" many asked. Boredom was not something I would come to know. When I mentioned my passion for stained glass making and how I couldn't wait to lose myself in my studio, they seemed convinced. The world of creating stained glass pieces began in my mid thirties. My career was process and idea focused, rarely demonstrating concrete results. My days called for balance and desire to make something with my hands. Something I could touch, see, and feel a sense of gratification in its completion. I experienced happiness and joy when making Tiffany style lamps and windows. Objects I would see in a magazine or art fair inspired me to create my own unique pieces. Friends and family reaped the rewards of the final products and this gave me immeasurable joy.

Stained glass was grounded in my religious years. Hours were spent beneath their dominant beauty, their reflections in the early morning light and in the soothing shadows of evening. My tools were the same used since the beginning of stained glass art: sketches and final designs, pattern cutting scissors, rows of glass arranged by color, standing next to one another, calling to be chosen for just the right texture or hue, glasscutters the size of a pencil, breaking pliers, copper foil or lead came, soldering irons. Bottles of chemicals like cutting oil and flux and patinas stained with their own identity lined the shelves, without which nothing would ever happen.

Before her retirement Robin absconded with an x-ray viewing box from her hospital that was being replaced by digital images. The guys in engineering re-wired it for her. This became my light box for viewing glass before the final selection. Each step was different and each dependent on the one preceding. Like the journey of life, planning is essential but you have to take it step by step, year by year and believe that all the pieces will come together. I loved the order of stained glass and through it the creation of something beautiful.

We don't see ourselves as others see us.

People would say to me, "You're so talented. You are an artist."

I never saw myself that way. I just loved the glass and the skill I had acquired. In later years I came to appreciate the discipline it takes and the love required to create the beautiful lamps and windows.

Mother Nature descended on Long Island in December of 2011 with a vengeance. Robin leaped from bed on that morning with the forecast of the previous night on her mind. She raised the blind of our bedroom window overlooking the long and steep driveway to our home. "We are not going anywhere today. It's at least two feet deep."

"I've got to call work. No way am I driving. Yea!" I yelled.

"This is the beginning of a long winter. It's twenty-five degrees out. Beautiful right now but how are we going to get down the driveway when it ices over?"

We laughed at the incident last winter when I fell on black ice at the bottom of the driveway. I flipped into the air and could not get back up on my feet.

It was scary but all I could do was laugh, making it more impossible for me to stand. Robin threw me a garden hose and pulled me up the driveway. More laughter.

The trees were weighted down; their branches ready to break away. The blue jays were hiding and chipmunks were prisoners in their holes, satisfied with their supply of peanuts for the winter.

We sat on the porch bundled up in our winter coats, enjoying our coffee and the brevity of this winter paradise, soon to turn into heavy, dirty slush and then solid ice.

"Maeve, what are we doing here? Let's go to Florida for a few weeks. We don't have to deal with this anymore."

"I'll get the time off. Just a few more months and I'll be totally free."

We visited friends near Tampa who had very convincing arguments for us buying property on the West coast.

At one of our early-bird outdoor dinners on the water, Eileen remarked how the snowbirds come and take the blue sweetener packets from the tables, leaving the white sugar packets.

"How do they know the difference?" I asked.

"Oh, you don't know what snowbirds are," she said with a big grin. We laughed as she explained and Robin chuckled to herself. I was a little embarrassed. Little did we know that before we got back on the plane, we would have made an offer on a villa in the lovely walking town of delightful Dunedin. And by next winter we would have officially become snowbirds ourselves, fluttering down to the sunshine state with all the other birds escaping the winters in the North.

There we were, climbing the mountain of accumulated years together. Suddenly we were in the last phase of life.

I was not expecting you so soon. I'm not ready. You'll have to wait.

Chapter 22

We shall not cease from exploration

And the end of all our exploring

Will be to arrive where we started

And know the place for the first time.

T.S. Eliot

Life is about choices. We travel on roads with detours, twists and turns and sometimes blind alleys. We can choose the smoothly paved road with signs to guide us, or we can choose the pebbled path, the rocky hill, the break in the woods. We live our choices, good, bad or indifferent. We come to crossroads and we set a new destination.

"How will we live our elder years, our well-earned retirement years?" I asked Robin as we embarked on our first twenty-four hour drive to Florida.

"Shall we sit and watch the sunsets over the Gulf of Mexico, drink margaritas and wait it out until the end arrives?" I took advantage of my captive driver and dramatized our future.

"Just imagine the sunsets with spectacular shades of gold and salmon, stretching and melting into each other until the red-hot center falls beneath the horizon. We can have our breath taken away as we did when we were young, seeing a Monet painting for the first time. We can feel lucky to witness such beauty. Lucky to be snowbirds basking in life with our Florida friends, plotting to make early bird dinners and happy hour."

"At days' end we can collapse on the bed, wondering how we got through another day of adventure. We can laugh at our ability to grab life by the gonads, to explore the world and enjoy our freedom," she said.

"Rocking by the fire or gazing at the sky each night is not for us. Our bodies are aging, but inside we feel like forty year olds. Living with gusto is not a way to avoid the inevitable. None of us are getting out of here alive," I said.

"No, but we'll have a hell of a time getting there," she said.

I remembered a class on developmental stages in life at New York University while getting my Master's Degree. The professor asked us to pretend to be old. Some students slumped in their seats, another began talking to herself, and another shuffled across the classroom floor. I couldn't morph into anyone other than my current self. I imagined my future to be strong. So I sat. I smiled and looked at the ceiling tiles, and the cracks forming on the marbleized linoleum floor. I touched the desktop and traced the etched lines made by those who sat before me. I stretched my body as long as I could beneath the undersized wooden desk and wrote the words on paper, "I'll be the same me with wrinkles."

A variation of the *To Do List* is the *Bucket List,* for all those places you want to visit, things you never did, but wished you had, new skills and new friends and perhaps re-visiting the past.

Travel took us to the mysterious Galapagos Islands whose landscape and inhabitants adapted and survived through millions of years. The Grand Canyon found us screaming for our lives as we rafted over the rapids. Robin jumped from a twenty-four foot cliff into the Colorado River.

"Oh no, she jumped too close to the rocks," said the guide.

Her head emerged as she fought the current away from the side of the mountain. Chap Stick, energy bars and pride flushed out of her pockets.

"I'll never do that again," she said when she reached land. "I'm glad I did it though."

Standing on an Alaskan glacier left us speaking in hushed tones as though we were in church.

"Do you realize we are whispering?" I asked her.

"We are, aren't we? Wow."

And there is always Ireland, sitting out in the Atlantic, calling me home.

It's strange that I still think of going home when I think of Ireland, almost sixty years after leaving as a child, but I do. This time I return in my late sixties, married to a woman and a convert to Judaism. Changed, but not really.

Robin and I rented an apartment in Westport, twenty minutes from Derradda. Westport is a cosmopolitan city with nightlife surrounded by beautiful countryside. Our windows faced Clew Bay with its 365 islands nestled between hills of grazing sheep.

Ireland is the easiest place in the world to return to, carrying memories and placing them for a few moments in the very spots they belong.

I stood barefoot in the bog with a soft Irish mist falling all around. The field of spongy wetness squeezed through my toes once again. It was here the bog claimed my nine-year-old shoes when I slipped into it years ago. I spread my arms to the sky as I laughed and did a dance of joy. Timmy, now a man and owner of the field looked on, bemused at the antics of his American cousin, dwelling in the memory of childhood.

I watched Timmy's grown son Eamon demonstrate the quickness and ability of his sheepdogs. Piercing whistles blew over the very hill where I destroyed the oat field by rolling down it as a kid. Eamon, yelled "Away to me, away to me," followed by a few whistles, and a small group of sheep landed a foot away.

I witnessed the home in Derradda filled again with mischievous children, jumping through the schoolhouse wall and gleefully getting into trouble. Those adventures, as simple as they were when we were nine, made life exciting and tapped into our fertile imaginations. It was happening all over again with two little boys. A third boy had just been born a week before, still safely cradled in his mother's arms, unaware of all the adventures awaiting him.

Four-year-old Nate, when he got up each morning, asked himself, according to his mother,

"What can I do to get into trouble today?"

He was fearless. Everything in his path was a challenge. The visiting Americans were easy prey.

"Step in it," he commanded as we both stood beside a large deposit of sheep shit in a field.

"I'm not stepping in it," I replied, amused by his boldness, staring up at me.

"Then I will," he said and poised his little foot just to the edge of the brown pile, waiting to be admonished. I laughed and he ran off.

We walked on the roads by the old well, around the fields bordered by stonewalls, constant and unchangeable. A section of old train track was different. It was replaced by the Greenway, a miles-long scenic walkway that ran right through Derradda. Tourists and locals bike and walk, inviting all to embrace this beautiful countryside.

Nine year-old Colin caught up to us on his bike.

"I was told to come down and get ye," he said. "Mam has dinner ready." He then proceeded to call a horse over from the end of a field so we could touch him.

"I bet ye don't have this in America," he said with pride.

"No. There's no place like this," I said.

The town of Newport is situated about three miles from the crossroads in Derradda. The Black Oak River runs through its Seven Arches Bridge, while Saint Patrick's Church, perched on top of a hill, proclaims its dominance over all. A three-bay stained glass window, titled *The Last Judgment* by Harry Clarke, Ireland's greatest stained glass artist, added the final message of awe for all who kneeled before it. Every Sunday we piled into the car, dressed in our best clothes for Mass at Saint Patrick's Church. Our thoughts focused on the ice cream afterwards in Brady's Pub where we eavesdropped on adult stories amid tea and rounds of Guinness. We rode our bikes or walked into town as children and hitch hiked as young adults. The town retained its historical character, except for the addition of a new hotel, gift shop and restaurants.

This visit I planned a Mass to be said remembering Bridget Walsh and James Walsh who left Ireland many years before. I, as a gift bearer, carried the water and wine to the priest down the long center aisle during the Offertory of the Mass. I placed them in the priest's hands, as I had done many times in earlier years. My religious beliefs had matured. I accepted the symbolism.

"Pray, my sisters and brothers that this sacrifice being offered, along with our very lives, are acceptable to God, the Almighty," the priest intoned.

My metaphorical journey through religion flashed before my eyes.

Am I stepping back in time or coming full circle?

After dinner at The Idle Wall on Clew Bay one evening, Mary, my cousin, Robin and I continued reminiscing.

"Maeve, do you remember the time we had a funeral for the dead crow right before you left Derradda for America?"

"I do. He was on the ground by the barn, lifeless. I remember his iridescent black feathers still glistening and wet from the rain. His yellow beak was wide open."

"Well you insisted we have a proper funeral. We placed him in a Cadbury biscuit box on top of a sheet of moss we lifted from a stone. We told Timmy he had to dig the grave in the backfield and attend the service. We had a procession and you presided over the service, saying prayers from Mass. We put a small cross on the grave. Do you remember?"

"Yep, I do. We put small stones all around it. I don't know why I did that. To you, it was natural to see a dead bird on the ground. To me it was traumatic."

"I think you were so sad because you were leaving Ireland, maybe. I don't know.

You were moved to do it, anyway. And we joined you."

"I really feel awful about never locating my grandfather's and younger brother's grave in the Castlebar cemetery," I said.

"Remember when we searched in the rain a few years ago and couldn't find it? I don't want it to be lost forever."

"Well, we have plenty of time this visit. Let's go one day and the three of us will look for it again. I know it's there," said Mary, always up for a challenge.

"Really? I would love to."

The next day we set out like CSI agents on a mission in the immense graveyard. It was a surprisingly cold day for late fall.

I suggested, "Let's spread a wide net by walking in separate lines so we cover a large area of gravesites."

I was not optimistic but had to give finding the Walsh graves one more honest-to-goodness try. I pulled my collar up to stop the wind from going down my neck as I checked each marked stone along my path. Ten minutes passed. Robin yelled from the highest point of our graveyard sweep, "Maeve, come here. Mary, Maeve."

"Come over here," she yelled again.

We ran to her and there it was, the headstone barely readable, the ground covered in brambles. Thorny vines pushed through the old stone and split it in half.

"This is it," I said, overjoyed. I hugged Robin and Mary. "This is it." I looked at Mary's black jacket to see light snowflakes landing on her shoulders.

"It's snowing," I said in absolute amazement. Feathery flakes gathered on the moss green graves. Snow once again arrived unexpectedly in Ireland to anoint, to solemnize the moment. Now I can bring the grave back to life and honor my grandfather and my brother whom I never knew. This will be done for my parents, for the Walsh family and for me.

I stood in the present, in the middle of where I originated. I arrived where I started.

Changed in many ways from all my exploring, I sat and stopped and listened.

Silence. Snowy silence. And then I heard the whispers in the wind. I heard the whispers in my heart. The most adventurous journey had been taking place within me. An adventure that demanded the most courage, the most honesty, the most self-revelation. A journey that recognized fear and rejection but smiled back and moved forward. A time of self-delusion replaced with simple clarity. A place of woundedness healed. A journey that continues with the possibility of forgiveness and the force of love.

11 92

RECEIVED SEP 1 7 2019